Homestead Sanctuary

K. L. BEASLEY

Fulton Books, Inc.
Meadville, PA

Published by Fulton Books 2020

ISBN 978-1-64654-924-5 (paperback)
ISBN 978-1-64654-925-2 (digital)

Printed in the United States of America

This book is dedicated to Picasso, a rescued paint horse, who I met while she was recovering from horrible abuse. Our time together may have been short, but our souls became one. Even in death, you made me promise to return to writing. This is the story you wanted to tell.

Contents

Acknowledgments

I would like to thank my beta readers, Sue and AJ, for their encouragement and good advice. I would like to thank Randy's Rescue Ranch and all the volunteers for showing me what a loving place a rescue ranch could be and for all the laughter and heartache we shared.

Most of all, I would like to thank my wife, Cheryl, for putting up with my crazy ideas, for encouraging me to follow my dreams, for the time and patience while writing this book, and for the love we share on this journey called life.

PART 1

The Beginning

CHAPTER 1

Alex, My Story

Wow, where do I begin? Has it really been five years since I returned to Montana? Through all the good and bad, I have always called the Kalispell area home. I have been deployed across the world for ten-plus years, but there is something to be said for coming home under any circumstances. I guess the first thing I should tell you is a little about myself for you to understand how Homestead Sanctuary came to life.

My name is Alex. I was born in 1982 and was raised on a quarter horse ranch that my dad and my uncle owned. I think I was riding horses before I learned to walk. I was breaking horses by the time I was fifteen, and I always imagined myself carrying on the family business. I also love to cook. Mom would let me "experiment" with anything we had on hand. There were a few disasters, like the hot dog lasagna, but most of the time, it was edible. Eventually, I figured enough of it out and could host a fairly good dinner party. Of course, that usually consisted of Mom and Dad, Uncle Bill, and Grandma and Grandpa.

Living outside town, I really did not have a lot of extracurricular activities, but I was okay with that. I was always able to come home to the horses, and it was there I always found my peace. We had anywhere from fifty to two hundred horses at a time. Most were quarter horses that we would train for the ranchers across the west, but occasionally we would have a few Appaloosas mixed in. I was always taken with the underdogs. Those that were rejected by their mom or got injured became my responsibility, and I honestly loved taking care of them.

After graduating high school in 2000, I planned on majoring in equine science when I attended Montana State University in the fall. Unfortunately, the fall brought several forest fires to the region, and as a volunteer, I spent much of August on a fire line, protecting Lolo National Forest.

CHAPTER 2

Mom

It was a blessing that I decided to delay my start at the university because in October my mom was diagnosed with stage 4 breast cancer. What I witnessed over the next five months was the complete transformation of my mom. After the surgery and the chemotherapy, she was a mere shell of herself. She was never a big woman, but during those six months, she lost so much weight and could barely get out of bed. I watched my dad hold it together day after day and often walked in on him crying in one of the barns. I never let him know I was there. I simply turned away to give him some space. He needed his time, just as I needed mine. I took on all the cooking and cleaning and found other chores to occupy my hands and my mind. But somehow, each evening I would find myself back with the horses.

Mom and Dad had one of those fairy-tale romances. They were high school sweethearts who married right after high school. To hear them tell the story, I was not planned, but they both were so excited when they found out Mom was pregnant. They had been living in the farmhouse with Grandma and Grandpa, but Dad wanted a home of their own before I was born. The nine-hundred-acre ranch had been in my family for generations, so Dad built a cabin on the back fifty acres with the help of my Uncle Bill and Grandpa. It was not a large cabin, three bedrooms and two baths, but it did have two barns. I seemed to always be dragging home strays.

I remember a neighbor showing up with a big horn lamb. Someone had hit the mom up near Glacier National Park, and the poor lamb was left all alone. He knew that I always took care of the young ones and asked if I could care for it. Of course, Mom and Dad did not say a thing as I carried it out to the barn to fix it a bottle. It was just the way it was back then. We lived in the cabin up until Grandma and Grandpa died in 1991 and 1993. My Uncle's house was on the north side of the property, and since he never married, he had no use for the big house and generously gave it over to us. It was a big farmhouse with a huge kitchen Mom had always loved. I can remember many summer nights sitting out on the wraparound porch, drinking lemonade, and watching the sunset. The cabin became a great hangout for the few friends I had and the occasional girlfriend. Being a teenager in Montana certainly had its advantages. Montana is one of the last forty-eight continuous states where the animal population is greater than the number of people.

By March we had brought hospice in for Mom. No one wanted to talk about it, but it was like the elephant in the room. We had brought a hospital bed into the guest bedroom on the first floor so Mom could look out the window when she was awake. She always loved the Montana sky, and she had a perfect view of the sunsets. I remember her calling me into the room just a few days before... well, you know. I still have a hard time saying it. She grabbed my hand and told me how much she loved me. She told me I was going to do great things in my life, and she would always be watching over me. She told me, whenever I needed her, I should find a two-tailed swallowtail butterfly and tell it of my wish, and that butterfly would carry my wish to her.

Mom was one-half Chippewa, and the Native American heritage had always been honored in our home. Mom passed away on March 18, 2001. As per the Chippewa customs, we lit a fire that burned for four days and nights. Her funeral was a mix of both Christian and Chippewa, and I was so proud of my dad for honoring my mom in such a way. He showed so much strength and compassion, and through it all, he never let the love for my mom dim in his eyes.

Someday I hoped to find that kind of love, the love that would carry you through the best and the worst. Mom was buried in the family cemetery located under the great pines on the northwest corner of the ranch. She was laid to rest, facing the sunsets she loved so much.

CHAPTER 3

Life Goes On

By mid-April, we had found our new normal at the ranch. Days were filled with new fillies and colts, and the air was just beginning to lose some of its bitterness. Once again, I was making plans to start MSU on August 27. I was both excited and scared, living away from home for the first time ever. Summer seemed to be a blur. Finally, I was all packed up and heading off to MSU. As I got ready to go, my dad gave me a hug and told me to learn a lot and come home soon. Uncle Bill gave me the "have fun but not too much fun" look, and I told them I would be home for Thanksgiving. Little did I know, things would change so dramatically.

On the morning of September 11, 2001, I woke to find out we were under attack. It was hard for me to imagine as I watched the Twin Towers fall. I had never been to New York, or any large city for that matter. Every television and every radio were tuned in. Everyone's computers were bringing us the latest news. I think everyone was in shock. Communications were sketchy at best, but I sent Dad an e-mail. Classes were canceled for the next few days, so Wednesday morning I packed up and headed for home. I was nineteen and thought the world had gone crazy.

I was so relieved to find Dad and Uncle Bill out working the horses. I could tell by their actions they were merely going through their routine, and their minds were elsewhere. Dad served in the Air Force for four years after he and Mom were married. Uncle Bill served eight in the Army. I think both were proud of their military service even though neither of them spoke about it.

At dinner that night I asked about their military history and what they did. Dad worked securing missiles while Uncle Bill was part of the 101st Airborne. They traded a few stories, and then Dad asked me why I had such an interest. I think he already knew the answer but was hoping he was wrong. I sat there, finishing my chicken, thinking of the best way to say what was on my mind. Finally, after the table grew so silent, I told them I wanted to enlist. I needed to do my part to defend our country. It was not a want but an actual need to be part of the bigger picture. I was hoping they would understand. Dad sat there quietly, waiting on me to say more. Uncle Bill asked me when I had come to this decision. I admitted I had thought about it for a while, but after Tuesday, I was determined. He asked what branch I was considering, and I told him I honestly did not know. Finally, my dad spoke. He said he would prefer that I did not go, but he asked me to do one thing.

He said, "If you finish your semester at MSU and still want to enlist, I will support your decision. But between now and then, you need to complete your studies and take a hard look at each military branch and decide what it is you want to do."

I thought about what he said, and I realized how much sense he made. I was nineteen and ready to run off to whomever would take me, and Dad reminded me I needed a plan. He wanted me to use my skills and make a sound decision.

The semester passed so quickly. I made it through all my classes, but my focus was still on which branch of the military I wanted to be part of and what I wanted to do. After talking to recruiters and completing all the other requirements such as the physical and the ASVAB, I was one step closer. I had taken the ASVAB in high school, but it was recommended I take it again. I was glad I did, as it showed an aptitude for imagery and intelligence analyst. I was hoping to get into the intelligence arena, so this was a great start.

Within a couple of months, I was off to Fort Leonard Wood in Missouri for basic training. The first few years in the Army were the same for most of us. After basic combat training, I attended sixteen weeks advanced training before being assigned to Fort Meade in Maryland. I was deployed as part of Operation Enduring Freedom in Afghanistan as well as Operation Iraqi Freedom. I will not go into detail, but there are parts of the war that will forever be burnt into the recesses of my mind. During this time, I was working in military intelligence and found I had the ability to pick up foreign languages. I learned how to understand and speak Farsi/Dari. I was no expert, but I could get by, so I found myself quite often being deployed to the region. Although it was difficult, I loved what I was doing. A far cry from my life in Montana, but what I was doing felt important. I had created another type of family, and we fiercely protected each other.

In 2014 I was assigned, as part of the American-led coalition, to provide extensive support to the Iraqi Security Forces. We were providing training, intelligence, and personnel. It was during this year my life changed forever. It was a simple training mission. Well, as simple as things got in Iraq. We were just outside Fallujah. It was July 29. The weather was hot, reaching one hundred degrees by the afternoon. We had been experiencing a few rain showers, a very welcome reprieve. While riding in a Humvee, an explosion occurred. We hit an IED or were hit by rocket. I still do not know for certain what is was, and the next thing I remember is being lifting into a helo. While unconscious, I had been triaged, transported to the airbase, and prepared to be airlifted. I do not remember much of the next few weeks. I know I was evacuated to Landstuhl Regional Medical Center in Germany before returning stateside to Walter Reed. It was in Germany where I first was able to comprehend my injuries. It was also where I learned about the death of my friends. I can write this now, but at the time, my mind just could not put the pieces together. I had lost my left leg, just above the knee, and lost most use of my left arm. I had lost three of my closest buddies. The Army notified my dad, and as soon as I was able, we visited by Skype. I do not think the realization had set in yet, but all I could remember Dad saying was I would be home soon.

It took eight long months of PT and both physical and mental evaluations before I was able to return to Montana. It was March 15,

2015, and it was cold—not the cold of my youth, when we could not wait to get outside and play, but more of the bone-chilling kind that felt like you were never going to get warm. Dad picked me up at the airport. I had managed to find a way to use crutches. I hated being stuck in a wheelchair. I really hoped in the next few months I would be fitted for a prosthetic. I had no idea what I was going to do with the rest of my life, but being stuck in a wheelchair was not an option. Dad had made a couple trips to Maryland during my rehab, but it sure felt good being back home with him. Uncle Bill was waiting for us when we got back to the ranch. He wrapped me in one of his bear hugs, but I could tell he was fighting back the tears.

After a few weeks, we had settled into a comfortable routine. I could manage getting up and making my way downstairs each morning, where Dad would always have something on the stove for me. I had lost weight and did not have much of an appetite. Dad along with Uncle Bill were usually already out with the horses, and I was left on my own to wander the house. How I envied them, going about life as they had for years. It was during this time I realized how much I had really lost. Like most veterans, my life could never be the same. The one thing I cherished the most, the freedom of riding the horses, was a distant past. The sense of loss was overwhelming at times. I realized my plan for the future was only a dream now. I would never be able to take over and run the ranch without significant help, and we did not make enough off the ranch to hire the help needed. Dad and Uncle Bill were not spring chickens, and the weight of the world felt as if it was resting on my shoulders.

I found myself often finding solace at the old cabin with a few too many beers. I was comfortable taking the gator, loading it with beer, and heading out. Sometimes I would stay out there all night. I knew I was feeling sorry for myself, but I did not know how to dig myself out of the hole. In May, on one of my trips to the VA, I was able to be fitted with a proper prosthetic. I was only allowed to wear it a few hours a day to start, but I worked hard to get my strength and my independence back. I had regained some use of my left arm, and I thought if I could walk, maybe I could figure out what I was going to do next.

CHAPTER 4

Ma Jolie

One evening in late August, while Dad and I were sitting out on the porch, Cody, our animal vet, came rumbling up the driveway in his old pickup truck. He wandered over to the porch and told us about a tragic fire that had taken place over by Whitefish. Apparently, a stable had been struck by lightning, and the horses had been trapped inside. He had just come from the property. The owners were in town, and by the time they got back, the stable laid in ruin. Cody told us he did not know how, but one of the paint mares had kicked so hard they had created a hole in the barn and then busted out. Ten of the horses had escaped with minor injuries, three did not make it, but the paint mare was severely burned and had sustained some major injuries to her leg. It looked like she had tried to go back in and save the others. The owners wanted Cody to put her down, but he was fighting them on it. He told them that she was the bravest damn horse he had ever seen, and she deserved a fighting chance. The owners agreed that if he found someone who was willing to take her in and cover her expenses that they would sign over ownership.

By the time Cody finished his story, I was fighting back the tears. Cody said he was willing to cover the expenses, but he needed to get her somewhere that she would be safe. He knew that I always took in the lost and injured animals back when I was a kid and was just hoping that maybe we would be willing to take in this mare. Dad looked at me, with that look only a dad can give, and told me if they brought her here, I would have to be the one to care for her. He and Bill were too busy with the ranch to play nursemaid to an animal that might not make it.

I turned to Cody and told him I was in no position to take on this critically injured horse, but he looked at me and said, "I thought that maybe you both could use the support and company, but I understand. I will keep looking."

I do not know if it was the sadness in Cody's eyes or my own desperation to feel useful, but I turned back to him and said, "Okay, I will try."

It took two days for the mare to be stable enough to try to bring her to the ranch. It took every bit of that time to get the old cabin and the barn ready for her arrival. I could not put her in with the other horses, and I thought back at the cabin would be a perfect place. I told Dad I was going to be moving into the cabin for a while to get her settled.

When Cody arrived with the mare, I was shocked. She smelled of sweat and smoke. Her once-white mane was an awful, dirty brown, and she had multiple open wounds and several stitched ones. The worst part was, her left leg was twisted in a fashion I could only describe as a twisted piece of metal. Her eyes told a story of a long-fought battle and showed just how tired she was. With Cody's help, we put together a form of a sling, allowing us to keep her upright and take the pressure off the leg. He had sedated her for the trip, and she could hardly put any weight on her injured leg. It wasn't looking good.

We had a supply of bute and Banamine on hand, as well as Wonder Dust and Wound Honey. Cody put together all the instructions I needed to care for her, including hydrotherapy to keep the wounds clean. He was coming back out to fully evaluate the injury to her leg later in the week. I brought in some fresh hay and grain and filled a bucket with nice, cool water. Dad had put a well in when he built the cabin, and I swear it is the best water I have ever drunk. I approached her slowly with the bucket and rubbed a little around her nose and mouth. When I placed the bucket on the ground, she nearly drained it. Well, that was a good sign for sure. I brought the grain close, and she took a few bites but looked at me with those big brown eyes that told me she wanted to sleep. I moved the hay within her reach and filled the water bucket once again.

I stepped outside with Cody so we could talk. I asked about her injuries and what he thought of her chances. Cody was never one to pull any punches. He said at best, she had a fifty-fifty chance. The fact she took some water and a little grain was a good sign. She had not done that the last two days. Cody told me that he would be back tomorrow evening to check on her, and he headed to his truck.

Before he pulled away, I yelled out to him, "Hey, what's her name?"

He said her former owners called her Ma Jolie, meaning "my pretty one." She was named after some famous painting by Picasso. Ma Jolie—I liked the name. I smiled to myself and headed back into the barn.

The first night I camped out in the barn. I wanted Jolie to get used to me being around. In honesty, it felt good to be needed. It was a restless night, and by morning I do not know how much sleep either of us got. The sun was shining, so I decided that today was going to be a good day. Since we rigged the sling up in the main part of the barn, there was plenty of room to try to clean Jolie up a bit. I went to the tack room, grabbing my grooming gear, and hooked the hose up to the water. I moved all the sawdust bedding out from around Jolie and found once again she had almost drained her water bucket. I was thankful Dad had always kept mats down in the barn, as it would make it easier for both of us.

I removed the bandages from around her injured areas to clean her wounds. I did not want to startle her, so I began with a cool trickle of water on one of her good legs. She seemed to relax into my touch as I thoroughly rinsed her injuries. I went inside for a bucket of warm water and returned with a sponge. As I started to clean her head, I realized she was a tricolored paint. It was hard to tell under all the dirt. When I looked into her eyes, it was as if there was a connection I could not explain. It was as if we could see into each other's soul. I could feel her pain, just as I felt my own.

As I continued with the grooming session, I used every comb and brush I owned. She seemed more relaxed as I continued to wash and comb out her mane and tail. When I finished drying her, I applied the various external meds and gave her pain meds. I rewrapped her injuries and took a step back. I was a mess and exhausted, but she looked beautiful. Her white mane and tricolored tail were shining. I still had a mess to clean up around the barn, and my leg was killing me, but I felt like I had accomplished something. It had taken me three hours to do something I used to do in thirty minutes, but I did it.

After finishing in the barn, including laying a nice fresh layer of bedding, I went inside to take a shower. I stood under the warm water as it beat down on my skin, and I seemed to be more aware of my body than I had for the past year. As I stepped out of the shower, I looked at myself in the full length. It was something I avoided doing. I saw my reflection, but it really was not me, at least not the me I remembered before the war.

I shook off my melancholy and reminded myself I still had a lot to get done. When I got dressed and towel dried my hair, I grabbed my crutches and headed back to the barn. I had kept my prosthetic on all day, and my leg was getting sore. As I entered, Jolie turned her head to me and gave me an approving nicker. As I looked into her eyes, I saw a twinkle that was not there before.

Moments later I heard a vehicle approaching. As I walked out of the barn, I saw Cody. He had brought a portable X-ray machine for us to check Jolie's leg. When Cody entered the barn, he looked at Jolie and then back at me. He shook his head in amazement. He could not deny the difference in her over the past twenty-four hours. After several X-rays and a thorough exam, we sat down with a couple of beers. He told me Jolie had a fracture in both the radius and the cannon, as well as several injuries to her ligaments and tendons. He was thankful there were no full breaks, but he was worried. He knew of a brace manufactured by Animal Ortho Care, but he had never used one. He thought it might help. We took several measurements, and he told me he would order it in the morning. In the meantime, he told me to keep doing what I was doing.

After I said goodbye to Cody, my stomach reminded me I had not eaten all day. I went back to the barn and made sure Jolie had grain and water then added some fresh hay. This was no easy task on crutches, but I quickly learned how to adapt. As I finished, I approached Jolie and laid my hand upon her neck. She turned, laying her head upon my shoulder. There we stood, both offering support to each other. I knew then and there, she was mine and I was hers. I turned on some music for her as I made my way to the cabin. It had been a good day, and I was hungry.

Early the next morning I heard someone enter the cabin. I was startled at first and reached for my gun.

Moments later, I heard my dad holler in at me, "Get your lazy ass up. I got something I need you to do."

A smile crossed my face. Yep, that was my dad, and he was done allowing me to feel sorry for myself. I threw on a pair of jeans, a T-shirt, and a cowboy boot then wandered into the kitchen. Dad had scrambled some eggs and had bread in the toaster. Coffee was brewing, and the sun was shining. We sat down at the kitchen table for a quick breakfast. He told me that he and Uncle Bill had been talking and thought it was about time I got more involved with running the ranch.

He said, "I know you can't ride, and it will take all of us to figure out what you can and can't do, but it's time. Bill and I ain't getting any younger."

After breakfast, Dad and I went out to the barn to check on Jolie. She was definitely more relaxed and more alert. He helped me with her feed and water, as well as all her wound care and meds, but left all the mucking for me. He was not going to let me take the easy road. When I finished, we hopped into his truck and headed toward the farmhouse. Bill was waiting for us. He laughed as we pulled up.

"Guess he wasn't letting your lazy ass sleep in today," he said as he wrapped me in a hug.

I shook my head and grinned.

There are many parts to running a horse ranch. The care of the horses would always first, then you had all the maintenance and repairs, dealing with potential buyers, checking all the tack and fence line, and of course, all the bookwork. The three of us sat down and decided, for the time being, Dad and Bill would handle the horses. We were down to about seventy head, and while the weather was still good, they were spending most of their time in the various pastures. We already had lined up buyers for about twenty before the winter set in. Dad liked cutting back to about thirty-five over the winter, knowing that in the spring, several of our mares would be giving birth. That meant we needed to find a buyer for around fifteen. I knew we had some nice riding horses, and I set out to find a buyer. I took on the responsibility for checking all the barns, ordering feed and hay, replacing any tack that could not be repaired, dealing with potential buyers, and of course, all the salesmen that showed up unannounced. I was also put in charge of any marketing.

Dad and Bill were not into social media. I had set up our website before I left and, thankfully, had a service monitoring it for us, but it was time for some updating. This was something I could do. I felt better than I had in a long while when I left the farmhouse that day. On the ride back to the cabin that afternoon, my dad asked me when I was going to start driving again. I had not really given it much thought. My truck was a stick shift, so I knew that was out of the question. I think he read my mind and told me tomorrow we were going truck-shopping.

When I arrived back at the cabin, I went to check on Jolie. She greeted me as I entered, as if asking about my day. After taking care of her, I made my way back into the cabin for a bite of dinner and a good night's sleep.

The next morning Dad was back bright and early. By the time we ate and took care of Jolie, it was time to head into Whitefish for some truck-shopping. Dad drove my truck just in case we found something. We talked on the way, and Dad wanted to know what kind of truck I wanted. I laughed and said I had no idea. He and Bill both drove Dodge Rams, so we headed there first. I think Dad saw me eyeing the Jeep Wrangler Rubicon when we pulled into the lot. We went over to the trucks, but he caught me looking back at the Wrangler. Finally, he said if I was interested in the Wrangler, we should go look. I told him no, I needed a truck if I needed to pull a trailer or something larger. He told me both he and Bill had trucks for that purpose, and both were automatics. He told me I should get something I wanted and something I would be comfortable driving. After a test drive, I drove out of Don "K" dealership with a new Jeep Wrangler. That's right, I drove. It felt so good to be driving again. It was worth celebrating, so on our way back through Kalispell, we stopped at Sweet Peaks for some salted caramel ice cream.

On Monday Cody called, and the brace for Jolie had arrived. He was planning on stopping by later in the day. I was telling Jolie that we had a surprise for her as I was taking care of her morning ritual. I was hoping we would finally be able to get her out of the sling. Her other wounds were healing, but she still refused to put weight on her leg. Around 4:00 p.m. I heard the crunch of tires on the gravel drive.

I stuck my head out of the barn to let Cody know where I was. He grabbed this long brace of metal and hinges. Jolie greeted Cody with a nicker. He explained to me the first thing we needed to do was to get the leg into a sleeve. I understood that well enough, as I had something similar for my leg. It took both of us everything we had to get it properly placed. He then showed me how the brace needed to be placed and tightened. After a few trial and errors, we had the brace on. The sling had been placed in a manner so we could gradually release the tension. It was time to see if she could stand on her own.

I slowly started releasing the sling while Cody kept an eye on Jolie. I could feel, more than see, Jolie's hesitation about putting weight on her leg. We continued releasing it slowly until she was standing under her own weight. After releasing the sling, we moved it to the side. It was the first time I got a good look at her. She stood about fifteen to fifteen and a half hands and probably weighed nearly one thousand pounds.

She was standing but still had not taken any steps. I took the lead rope from Cody and looked into the now-familiar brown eyes. I wanted her to know we would do this together. The first steps were very tentative, but as we moved closer to the doors, I felt her confidence growing. As we stepped outside into the sunshine, I looked back over my shoulder at Cody. He was snapping a photo with his phone that I still have printed on our website today. I led Jolie over to the grass area, and as she lowered her head to graze, I could feel her gratitude. I cannot explain, but somehow, we were connected; we were one.

For the next couple of months, we fell into a routine. I would get up, take care of myself and Jolie, check in with Dad and Bill, handle the books and marketing from the cabin, then take a break. Every afternoon, weather permitting, I would take Jolie out for a long walk around one of the back pastures. She was gaining strength and regaining the muscle tone she had lost. I noticed the same changes taking place in my own body.

By mid-October we had already received a few snowstorms, and the cold was settling back in. Cody stopped by each week to check on Jolie, and we had been slowly giving her time without the brace in the barn. It was finally time to remove the brace entirely, but Cody cautioned she still was not ready to run, so I needed to keep her on lead. That was a welcome relief.

The ranch was doing well. I had found buyers for the fifteen horses, we had several more inquiries for the spring, and the remaining horses were safely tucked into the main stables. I often would go up to the farmhouse to have dinner with Dad and Bill, most of the time doing the cooking. I still enjoyed it, and it was nice seeing Dad and Bill.

CHAPTER 5

Tapaguer

One evening in late October, I was returning from the farmhouse, and I noticed something moving ahead of me. There was snow on the ground, and it was cold outside. I could not quite make out what it was at first, so I stopped. Cautiously I got out of the Jeep while keeping the headlights pointed on the slowly moving mound. By now I could tell it was an animal, but I was not sure yet just what kind it was.

As I got closer, I heard the distinct growl and immediately knew it was a dog. The growl was certainly more of a scared growl and not one of aggression, but I still knew I had to be careful. I approached slowly, calmly talking to the dog. I was hoping that I could calm it down enough to get close. I then remembered I had left over chicken in the Jeep, so I went to grab it.

This time, as I approached, I tossed a few bits of chicken out to the dog. Hesitant at first, the dog finally moved to grab a piece. It was then I noticed it was some type of a retriever or retriever mix, and it was a she. Tucked in below her were at least three pups. I knew I had to get her to trust me so I could get her and her pups out of the snow and cold. I tossed another couple of pieces of chicken a little farther away, hoping she would move a little farther away from her pups. It worked, and I quickly grabbed two of the pups. Thankfully, I had my leg on still and had both hands free. She looked at me and growled, but I calmly spoke to her as I put the pups into the Jeep. I tossed some more chicken, but she had returned to the remaining pups and would not move. When I had grabbed the pups, I found there was a total of four. That meant I still needed to get the remaining two and mom. I grabbed my phone and called Dad. I asked him if he could bring Bandit, his terrier, and a slip lead out to me. I explained what was happening, and he said he would be right there.

About twenty minutes later he arrived and asked me what he could do to help. I asked him to take Bandit to the far side of Momma and then slowly approach. I anticipated she would attempt to get between Bandit and her babies. Luckily, I was right, and when she moved to protect her babies, I jumped in and grabbed the remaining two. Now to get Momma. I had all four pups in the back of the Jeep. I had Dad and Bandit go back over to his truck. I put a few more pieces of chicken in the back of the Jeep as well. I walked over to Dad and made sure Momma knew where we were. It took a while, but Momma could not resist the whine of her babies. Eventually, she jumped into the back of the Jeep, and thankfully, I was able to get the back end closed. I took the slip lead from Dad and told him I would meet him at the cabin. I cautiously got into the Jeep and found Momma still in the back with her babies.

When I got to the cabin, I drove straight into the main barn. Jolie was in her stall, so I was able to pull all the way in. Dad was right behind me, parking just outside. He left Bandit in the truck and closed the barn doors as he entered. We set up the far stall with some fresh bedding. Fortunately, Dad had thought to grab some dog food when he loaded up, so we put the food and some water down. We had a couple of old blankets in the barn, so we fixed up one corner of the stall and went to open the back end of the Jeep. When we opened it, Momma growled a warning but did jump down. Dad and I grabbed the pups and carried them over to the stall. Momma followed us at a safe distance, keeping a close eye on her babies. When we stepped out of the stall, Momma rushed in, sniffing each of them, ensuring we had not hurt them. I was able to close the stall door without a problem, and within a few minutes, Momma was lying down nursing her little ones. I thanked Dad and grabbed my phone to call Cody. Upon telling Cody my story, he agreed to come out tomorrow and check out the pups.

Through all the excitement, Jolie had stood by, head out her stall, just taking in all the action. I walked over and reached my hand up to her neck. I told her she had company and to keep an eye on them. She laid her head on my shoulder, something she had been doing frequently, and we both let out a deep sigh.

"Good night, my pretty one," I said as I got ready to exit the barn.

After backing the Jeep out and closing the barn doors, I said goodbye to Dad and headed into the cabin. I was wet and cold, but I was happy.

I was up early the next morning and went to check on the pups and Jolie. I took a little more of the leftover chicken with me, hoping to make friends with Mamma. When I entered, I tried to remain quiet. Jolie looked up from her stall and let out her good-morning nicker. I approached the stall with the pups to find Mamma curled up on the blankets and the pups eagerly nursing. She looked up at me but no longer growled.

I said, "Good morning, Momma."

With that, I got a wag of the tail. It was a start; I would take it.

As I was just finishing my morning chores, I heard the familiar arrival of Dad's truck. He wanted to bring down some more dog food and blankets, plus check on the pups. He also had some warm cinnamon rolls. Dad was not much of a cook, but boy, could he bake. I remember Dad liked to surprise Mom on the weekends by making up a batch of coffee cakes, cinnamon rolls, or homemade bread. I always knew when Dad was baking; the house smelled wonderful.

After grabbing a cinnamon roll and shoving it in my mouth, we headed to the barn. We shut the door behind us so we could open the stall door for Momma. We wanted her to understand she was not trapped.

We opened the stall door and then walked over to Jolie. She had already developed a sweet tooth because I had been treating her to some sugar cubes and peppermints. Most people do not know it, but horses love peppermints. She smelled the frosting from the cinnamon rolls on my face, and the next thing you know, she was giving my chin a little nibble. She did not actual bite, more of a lick with those big horse lips. Dad started laughing, and then so did I. We had not noticed Momma coming out of the stall until we both looked down. She was by my feet and wagging her tail. I slowly reached down and gave her a gentle pat. Things were going to work out fine.

Early afternoon, Cody managed to swing by. I took him out to the barn, and he immediately recognized Momma. Her name was Maggie, but he needed to check her microchip to be sure. He suspected she belonged to a family in Columbia Falls. He said Maggie was a golden retriever, and she had been stolen about six months ago. The family had been looking for her ever since. Maggie seemed to recognize him and allowed him to check her and examine her pups. There were two girls and two boys, and he estimated them to be about five weeks old. Other than being underweight, they all seemed to be healthy. Cody told me it was a good thing that I found them when I did. They would not have survived without my help.

After confirming Maggie's owners, Cody gave them a call. I could hear the screams on the phone. They had never given up on finding her and were absolutely thrilled she was safe. When he told them she had four puppies, I could hear the kids squeal in the background. We planned for them to drive over the next day, and we would go from there.

It seems while we were on the phone with Maggie's owners, she and Jolie were having a conversation of their own. Jolie had her head bent as far down as she could, and Maggie had her paws up on the stall door. I am not sure what they were discussing, but for some reason, it felt like they were talking about me and the cabin. Maybe I was just being a little paranoid.

After taking Jolie for our regular walk, I popped in to check on Maggie and the pups. She was finally comfortable enough around me to let me get close. I lowered myself down onto the floor to be comfortable. The runt of the liter was a little boy. He may have been tiny, but he was certainly the loudest. I reached over to pick him up. I brought him close to my chest, and he snuggled in immediately. He was not just the smallest but his coloring was so light he was almost white. The others looked more like Maggie, with the darker golden-retriever coloring. The other three seemed quite content to lay snuggled together, but every time I tried to put the little guy back with his brother and sisters, he would cry. I think Maggie was just as confused as I was. I finally had to get back to work, so I laid the little guy right next to Maggie, and he began to nurse. It was time for me to make my escape.

The next morning, I was up early. It seemed to be coming a habit lately. I grabbed a quick breakfast and headed to the barn. All was well with everyone, so I grabbed Jolie's lead and my coffee mug and went outside to sit on the old picnic table. Jolie grazed and I was finally able to really relax. I took a deep breath and really looked around. I was surrounded by such beauty: the mountains, the pines, the pasture, the snow...and one beautiful horse.

As I finished the morning chores, I saw Cody's truck arrive followed by a Subaru SUV. No sooner had the car stopped moving than two kids popped open their doors and ran toward me. Their mom and dad got out and yelled for the kids to calm down. Everyone was talking at once, and I could not help but laugh. Cody caught up to them and made all the introductions. Their last name was Murphy, and they explained how Maggie had been taken from their fenced in yard. The kids had been heartbroken, but they never gave up looking for her. No one could figure out how she had managed to get almost twenty-five miles from home and in the middle of our ranch.

The minute we entered the barn, Maggie ran to the kids. I am not sure who was more excited. All of us adults moved over toward the pups. The three were once again snuggled up, sleeping, but the littlest boy was making quite the ruckus of his own. I reached down and picked him up. He snuggled next to my chest again and calmed down almost instantly.

I offered Cody and the Murphys some lemonade and introduced them to Jolie, who was patiently waiting for some attention of her own. Cody retold the story of Jolie to the Murphys while I went for the lemonade. We sat at the picnic table and visited for a while. They were a nice family, and I was glad I was able to reunite them with Maggie and her pups.

When we had everyone—including Maggie and the pups—loaded up, it was time to say goodbye. Ed, the father, pulled me aside and told me he and his wife were just talking. They saw the connection I had to the little pup, and he wanted to know if, in a few weeks, when the pup was old enough, I would be interested in taking him. Cody was going to help in finding homes for all of them, and they wanted to give me first choice. I think a tear came to both of our eyes, and I told him I would love to take him. We exchanged phone numbers and e-mails, and he said he would be in touch soon. He told me I had better think of a name and, as soon as I had one picked out, to let them know.

Once the Murphys left, Cody went back over to get a good look at Jolie. He was so happy with the progress she had made. He reached out and put his hand on my shoulder. He let me know that he thought I was remarkable and thanked me for my service. He knew I had been struggling, but what I had done for Jolie and the pups was amazing. I shrugged it off and just said thanks, but it felt good; it felt right.

Later that night I was thinking of a name for my soon-to-be new pup. Since I had Jolie, a French word, I thought maybe I should come up with a similar process for the pup. The internet is a wonderful tool, and when I searched Google for a French word meaning "noisy," I found *Tapaguer*. That was it, Tapaguer—Tapa for short. I e-mailed Ed and headed off to bed.

The next morning, after getting the morning chores done, I sat down to do some work on the computer. I checked my personal e-mail and found a response from Ed. Apparently, he approved of the name since Tapa kept them up half the night with his whimpering. He said it was going to be a long three weeks. I just laughed, knowing he was right for both of us; it was going to be a long three weeks.

As promised, three weeks later, the Murphys were back. They were delivering three of the pups to their forever homes and keeping one of the girls for themselves. The minute they put Tapa on the ground, he made a beeline toward me. I scooped him up and held him close. He had grown but still nuzzled his way between my jacket and flannel shirt. He was home.

Thanksgiving was peaceful. I fixed dinner at the farmhouse for Dad and Bill. The rest of the winter was fairly quiet except for Christmas. I made sure all three houses had Christmas trees, and Dad, Bill, and I had a competition on decorating. My tree was decorated with more of a rustic look, Dad's was a traditional-looking tree, and Bill's was—how do I put this—it was like a tree you would picture if you were sitting in Key West, drink in hand, listening to Jimmy Buffet singing Margaritaville. There were pink flamingoes, little paper umbrellas, sandals, and tropical ornaments. Around the bottom he had sand. His living room was decorated in a beach theme, and he had beach chairs in place of his furniture. I have some wonderful Christmas memories, but I do not think anything can compete with this one. Dad and I both agreed, Bill won.

Cody stopped by several times over the next few months to check on Jolie and Tapa. He made sure he checked all our horses every couple of months and wanted to check on our pregnant mares. We had nine that were expecting, and for two of them, it would be their first foals.

CHAPTER 6

A Cry for Help

It was late February when I heard a truck coming down the drive after dark. That just does not happen out here in the middle of nowhere. It was not Dad, and it wasn't Bill. I knew the sounds of their trucks. I grabbed my gun and headed outside. It is harder for me to get around at night and in the dark, but I did not want whoever it was finding me unprepared. I maneuvered myself into a position by the door with my gun in my right hand and flipped on the porch light. The truck clambered to a halt right in front of me. I was blinded by the headlights momentarily.

I heard the driver door open, and then a voice hollered out to me, "Sorry, so sorry... I didn't know what else to do."

The headlights went off, and in front of me stood a kid; she could not have been more than seventeen. I could tell she was upset. Her face was tear streaked, and she certainly was not dressed for the weather. I motioned for her to come inside and sit down. I found out her name was Julie, and her parents have a cattle ranch on the other side of Kalispell. She said one of the cows had a calf, and the mom rejected it. She had been trying to get it to take a bottle, and it would not. Her dad was going to kill it, so she put it in her truck and drove here. Cody is their vet, and he had told her the story of Jolie and Tapa. She needed my help. All during the story Tapa had been leaning up against her, and she had been petting his head. Her tears had almost subsided by now, and then I realized what she had just told me.

"You have a calf in your truck?" I asked in disbelief.

She nodded her head yes. I grabbed my coat and headed for the door. While she had been telling me her story, I had unconsciously put on my leg. When I reached her truck, sure enough, tucked in the back seat was one of the smallest angus cows I had ever seen. I grabbed it in my arms and carried it inside. It was alive, but extremely cold. I threw some towels in the dryer to warm up and asked her what she had tried to feed him. She told me she had some multispecies replacement milk, but he would not take it. I grabbed my phone and called Dad. We always kept Foal-Lac milk replacement on hand for our foals, but I did not really know anything about cattle. He agreed to bring a couple of bottles and some Foal-Lac down. I told him I would explain when he got here. I grabbed the warm towels from the dryer and gave them to Julie. I told her to wrap the little one up in the towels so we could get its body temperature up. My next phone call was to Cody.

I reached his voice mail, but before I finished leaving a message, he was already calling me back. I explained what was going on, and I told him I had no idea what I was doing. He sounded relieved. Apparently, Julie's parents had called him and told him she had taken off with the calf, and they had no idea where she was. He was going to call her parents and let them know she was safe, and then he would be out. He had some Purina Nurse Pro 200 in his barn, and he would bring it with him. It was a medicated milk replacement for cattle, and we may be able to get him to take it in a bottle. If not, Cody would feed him with a tube.

Within fifteen minutes Dad arrived, and Bill showed up maybe ten minutes later. He was apparently upset about missing the last excitement, so Dad had called him. I told Dad that Cody was on his way and he did not have to stay.

He just laughed and said, "What, and miss all the fun?"

I introduced Julie to the guys, and within another twenty minutes, Cody came bounding down the drive. Once he made it inside, we all moved out of his way so he could get a look at the little calf. Cody gave me instructions on how to mix the milk replacement he brought and put it in the bottle. He tried repeatedly to get him to nurse but finally had to tube-feed him. It looked like it was going to be another long night.

About thirty minutes later, there was another vehicle heading down the driveway.

"Now what?" I asked to no one in particular.

It seems Cody not only told Julie's parents she was safe but he also told them where she was. I grabbed a couple more cups for coffee; the more the merrier.

After all the introductions, and getting Julie's parents calmed down, it was time for a serious discussion. Julie's dad wanted no part of the calf. He just wanted to grab Julie and get his family home. Julie did not want to leave. Dad and Bill just sat back to watch the show, and Cody was busy checking on the calf.

Finally, I had enough.

"Okay, this is how it is going to work," I said.

I told Julie's dad that I was fine with keeping the calf here and handling the medical expenses, but I was going to need some help if the calf was going to pull through. It would require round-the-clock feedings and a lot of attention. I told him that I would need Julie to help me out. I knew Julie would be happy to help, but I did not want to give her dad an option. I think I may have scared him a bit, but he agreed. I told him to take Julie home tonight and to call me by 7:00 a.m. If the calf was still alive, Julie would come out to relieve me. We exchanged phone numbers, and I sent them on their way. I took one look at Dad and Bill and shook my head. I told them to go on and head home. They both needed some rest, and they needed to be up early. They nodded and gave me a hug on their way out.

I heard Dad mumble to Bill on his way to the truck, "This place is turning into a dang sanctuary."

Bill just laughed and said, "Well, you know, this homestead has always been a sanctuary for us."

And this, my friend, is how Homestead Sanctuary began. I will follow this with more stories of the people and animals that have become such a large part of my life. There is more to come with Jolie and Tapa as well as the calf, but that is another story for another day.

Welcome to Homestead Sanctuary and all the madness to follow.

PART 2

Building Homestead

CHAPTER 7

Dakotah

I do not really know if I would consider Jolie or Maggie the homestead's first rescue. Heck, maybe it should be the other way around, and I am their first rescue. All I know for certain is that when I closed the door after Cody left, it really didn't seem so odd that was I sitting in the cabin with an Angus calf contemplating what it meant to operate an animal sanctuary.

Before Cody left, we talked for a while. We found the calf was male, and we took time to really look him over. He was solid black, except for one little spot of white on his chest. He was so tiny, weighing somewhere around thirty to thirty-five pounds. He was not yet standing on his own, and his eyes remained closed. Cody had to head home, but he told me he would be back by 8:00 a.m. If anything changed with the calf during the night, he would have his phone close by. He told me not to get my hopes up. Even though I heard his words, I already had my hopes focused on him making it. I tend to be the type that wears my heart on my sleeve when it comes to animals, and it was no different this time. If the calf made it through the night, Cody would show me how to tube-feed him in the morning.

After getting Tapa out to do his business, I took my leg off and lowered myself down to the floor. Wrapping the little guy in my arms, I tried to get some sleep. I was wedged between Tapa and the calf. It seemed like every hour I would wake up just to check and make sure he was still breathing.

I jumped when my phone rang about 6:30 a.m. It was Julie checking in. She was thrilled when I told her the little guy was still alive. She talked to her dad, and he agreed to let her come by for a while before she headed to school. I wanted to try to give him a bottle before anyone else arrived. I mixed the bottle just as Cody had instructed me last night. It was warm and reminded me of buttermilk. I tried getting him to drink, but he did not want to take it. I decided to give it one more try before Julie arrived. I turned on some music, grabbed a blanket to wrap around me, and then pulled him onto my lap, holding his head up with my left arm. Holding the bottle in my right hand, I pushed the nipple of the bottle into his mouth. I began messaging his neck, and suddenly I felt him take his first drink. I tried to stay calm, but I was so excited. One, two, and then three swallows. It was working. He didn't take all of it, but it was a start. He finally opened his eyes. Although I had not spent much time around cattle, I was sure that I had never seen a cow with blue eyes. The iris was a pale blue, and the periphery was a tan color. He stared at me, just as I stared at him.

Moments later I heard a truck. I was certain it was Julie, so I just yelled out and told her to come on in. She tentatively opened the door and walked in. Seeing me on the floor she instantly started to shake. I shook my head and motioned for her to come over to where I was sitting. He turned his head to look at her, and when their eyes met, my heart soared. I could see the love between them. I asked Julie what she wanted to name him. She was surprised and told me I should pick out the name, but I told her, "You saved him, you have to name him." I told her to think about it, and she could let me know later.

I filled Julie in on what had been happening, and we sat down to figure out a feeding schedule. Julie could come by in the morning and then after school. For now, he would need to be fed every four hours, so Julie would take the 7:30 a.m., 3:30 p.m., and the 7:30 p.m. That left me with the 11:30 a.m., 11:30 p.m., and the 3:30 a.m. schedule. There would not be much sleeping over the next few months.

Cody arrived just before 8:00 a.m., as Julie was heading out for school. She was all smiles and gave both of us a huge hug before she jumped in her truck. As Cody and I walked into the cabin, I mentioned the unusual blue eyes. Cody was a bit surprised but said it was not unheard of. It was a condition called oculocutaneous hypopigmentation (OH). It was caused by a recessive gene passed on by his parents, and other than possibly having a sensitivity to light, he should not have any other issues. When I told Cody I was able to get the calf to take a bottle, he smiled. He told me if anyone was going to get a bottle down him, it would be me. He checked the calf over and told me that if he took the bottle at 11:30 a.m. that we should probably move him out to the barn. We headed over to the barn so I could take care of Jolie and to let her know our walk would be delayed today. Somehow, I think she understood something was going on and just nodded her head when I gave her the news.

Cody could not stay for long; he had another patient to check on. As soon as he left, I made sure Tapa got outside to do his business and then headed for the shower. I was stiff and sore. My leg was throbbing, and I still had phantom pains. After my shower, I laid down for a bit. I called Dad to update him and then set my alarm for 11:00 a.m.

About 10:00 a.m. I heard my phone notification, telling me I had a text. I was surprised to see it was from Julie. She had been thinking about the calf all morning and had told her friends about him. If it was okay with me, she wanted to call him Dakotah. She told me her great-great-grandfather was a member of the Dakotah tribe. She had heard the name Dakotah meant ally or friend.

I responded by telling her I thought that would be perfect and then went to check on him. I found him standing up, with a blanket draped over his head and back.

I let out a laugh and said, "Well, hello, Batman."

Tapa had not left his side and let out a bark of his own, as if reminding me he was there. I reached over and picked him up as he nuzzled into my chest.

A little later Dad stopped by to check on everything and to help me get a stall set up. He had run into town and picked up some bedding made from corncobs. It was a little cleaner than the shavings, and we wanted him to have a clean environment. We hooked up a couple of heat lamps and put the blankets down to give him something familiar in the stall. We half-walked, half-carried Dakotah into the stall and made sure he was comfortable.

Jolie looked on with interest while Tapa continued to play around my feet. I had a little while before Julie was due back, so I decided to take Jolie out for a walk. There was too much snow for any grazing, but I wanted to make sure we kept working on her leg strength. Tapa loved the snow, so he gladly jumped along with us as we walked.

When Julie returned, I was researching what steps and forms I would have to do to register Homestead Sanctuary. She anxiously exited her truck. When she entered the cabin, she came to a dead stop. I had not told her we had moved Dakotah, and she freaked out. Once I calmed her down and told her where he was, she ran to the barn. By the time I arrived, she was already in the stall with her arms wrapped around him. With just a little instruction, Julie had his bottle ready and sat down to feed him. I left her to it and told her to catch up with me before she left.

It was about an hour later she came up to the cabin. She was so happy. She reached down to pet Tapa and told me she cleaned up the stall. I asked if she wanted to join us for dinner up at the farmhouse, but she told me her dad had been adamant about her being home for dinner. She said she would be back by 7:30 p.m. I grabbed Tapa, and we headed up to the farmhouse. It was a spaghetti kind of night, and I still had some sauce tucked away in the freezer from the last time I made it. When Dad and Bill got in from the stables, I already had dinner cooking. They had been checking on one of the pregnant mares. It was going to be her first foal, and she seemed to be getting close.

We filled each other in on our day, and they both followed me back out to the cabin after dinner. Dad and Bill went over to see Dakotah, and I headed over to Jolie. I was exhausted, and Jolie seemed to share her energy with me. As soon as Dakotah's stall was open, Tapa went running into him. When Julie arrived, she showed

Dad and Bill how to mix a bottle, and Dad told me to go in and go to bed. He and Bill would hang out at the cabin until the 11:30 feeding and then make sure Tapa was taken care of before they left. I was too tired to argue, and I knew the 3:30 a.m. feeding would come too soon. Julie asked if it would be okay to bring a friend out with her the next day, and I told her that would be fine.

CHAPTER 8

Normal Until...

Over the next several weeks, we fell into a semi-normal routine. Julie was able to help more on the weekends, and her mom and dad even found time to make an appearance. Dakotah was growing, and we were able to reduce his feedings from every four hours, to every six hours, and then to every eight hours. He and Tapa were almost inseparable during the day, but at night, Tapa still liked to snuggle on my bed.

I had managed to supply all the paperwork needed to get Homestead Sanctuary set up as a 501(c) and applied for a business license. Since the main ranch already had a current inspection from the Department of Agriculture, Danny, our local inspector, came by and made sure I had the cabin and barns in order so he could issue his inspection form as soon as I received the license.

During this time, we had also added a couple of donkeys that we affectionately named Pinky and Brain. Danny had been notified that these donkeys were running wild down by Bigfork. He reached out to Cody and asked for his help in getting them. I had no idea any of this was happening until I heard Cody pull up in the driveway with a trailer in tow. Both donkeys were on the small side, but not what would be considered miniature. Brain was solid gray and was obviously in charge. Pinky was brown and white and was very laid back. If fact, Danny said when he and Cody finally tracked them down and opened the trailer, Pinky wandered right up to them to see what was going on. Brain, on the other hand, was able to avoid them for almost four hours.

We were able to get them settled into the main barn with Jolie and Dakotah. I think Jolie was enjoying the company, and I always made sure that we had our own time together. She kept me grounded, and anytime I felt stressed, all I needed to do was take a walk with her.

It was late April when I woke around 3:00 a.m. I don't know how or why, but I knew beyond a doubt there was something wrong at the barn. Jolie had woken me and told me. I did not question it. I jumped up, grabbed my crutches and my gun, and headed for the door. Tapa tried to push through the door, but I held her back. I switched on the lights and headed for the barn. As I approached, I did not initially notice anything. I opened the door and found all the animals standing and obviously distressed. I looked around the inside and found nothing out of place. I spent a few minutes calming them all down and thanking Jolie for alerting me. As I stepped outside and closed the door, I found it. In my hurry to enter the barn, I had completely missed the bear prints in the snow and the claw marks on the large barn doors. I could not get a good look in the darkness, but it appeared the bear had gone. I checked the barn one more time and then headed over to the cabin. I double-checked the doors, but I wasn't able to fall back asleep.

As soon as it was daylight, I reached out to Dad and Bill. They were going to head out to check the stables right away. I also reached out to Julie to tell her to be careful when she came out and then reached out to Montana Fish and Wildlife. I had to leave a message since no one was available yet, but after leaving a detailed message, I went to see the barn in the daylight. Just in case, I put a lead on Tapa, and we headed out. When we reached the barn, I could see how desperate the bear was to get into the barn. I put Tapa inside with Dakotah and then walked around the entire perimeter. There were bear prints and claw marks on every side. I also noticed several puddles of blood, so it appeared the bear was hurt.

Bears are fairly common in Montana, but they typically avoid human contact. I could not tell you the last time we had any bears wander near the ranch. Fish and Wildlife called me shortly after I got back inside the barn and told me they would be out sometime today. I told them what I had discovered and asked if they could bring a bear trap out. As much as I did not want a bear around the animals, I also didn't want anyone killing the bear.

By late afternoon, we had everything in place. I asked Julie to always come to the cabin before going to the barn. Fish and Wildlife brought out a bear trap and had set it up near the tree line and had bait inside. Dad and Bill said everything was good at the stables, and all the animals had seemed to calm down.

When we sat down to dinner that night, Dad asked me if I had heard the bear and if that was what woke me up. I looked at him and knew, no matter how crazy it sounded, I needed to tell him the truth. I told him that I had been sound asleep and that Jolie had somehow entered my head and warned me something was going on. Dad just nodded his head. He told me Mom was very connected to horses and had been her whole life. He believed in her abilities and was not surprised I had the same connection with Jolie.

The first night I sat awake in the dark, listening for any signs of trouble. By the third night, I figured the bear had moved on, so I headed to bed, not worrying about it. Early the next morning, as I opened the door to head to the barn, I heard a loud ruckus. The bear had been caught in the trap. I contacted Fish and Wildlife to let them know, and they said they would be out shortly. I was a bit surprised when Cody pulled in a little while later. He informed me Fish and Wildlife had called him and asked if he could come out to tranquilize and check on any injuries the bear might have.

A few hours later, we had a tranquilized grizzly bear laid out on the small barn floor, and Cody was checking on his injuries. Upon examination, he had been shot and, at some point, had a paw caught in a trap. Once Cody finished treating him, we loaded him up in the transport, and Fish and Wildlife would attend to his care. Within a few days, they would return him to the wild in a remote part of Glacier National Park.

CHAPTER 9

Building a Family

With the weather warming up and the extra animals, Cody suggested that I might want to add a few volunteers to help around the sanctuary. There is a lot to do on the ranch this time of year, and now with the sanctuary, the work had nearly doubled. I asked Julie to check with her friends from school to see if anyone might want to volunteer. I also listed the opportunity on a few employment internet sites.

It was through one of these sites I received a call from a gentleman named Jerry Graham. He told me that he was moving his father into a retirement community because he was unable to stay at his farm all alone. Jerry and his family lived near Bozeman, and there was no one nearby to check in on him. During our conversation, he informed me his dad had mild dementia, and the family would be selling the farm. I found out his dad's name was Joe, and he was seventy-three. Jerry said his dad had a horse on the farm that was about twenty years old, and his dad had owned him since he was two. On good days, his dad was adamant he was not leaving the farm, but Jerry knew he had reached a point that they had no option. The reason for his call was, he was hoping I would be willing to take in his dad's horse. His was hoping if the horse was close by, maybe his dad could come and visit. He thought that might make the move easier on his dad. I told him I would consider it, but I would really like to meet him and his dad first. He provided me the address of the farm, and I agreed to meet him out there on Saturday afternoon around 1:00 p.m.

When I arrived at Joe's farm, Jerry met me in the driveway. I was glad that he did because I had a question for him before I met Joe. I asked if Joe was still driving. Jerry told me he was, but he was not sure for how long. He did tell me the retirement community had a van and often took the residents shopping, on outings, or to appointments. I thanked him, and we went inside. Joe stood up when I entered and gave me a once-over. You know, that look someone gives you when they are trying to size you up. I reached out to shake his hand and told him how much I appreciated him taking time to speak to me. He shook my hand and just nodded.

His first comment to me was, "I understand you are wanting to take Kodiak." His next was, "What happened to your leg?" The one thing with older people—they tend to lose their filters. I actually appreciated his directness and explained to him what had happened. I had been thinking about how I could handle this situation regarding the horse, and I had some ideas. I asked Joe to tell me a little bit about Kodiak. He told me Kodiak was about twenty years old, and he had gotten him from a ranch just outside town. He said "them fellas" raised quarter horses. He was looking for a new horse and was willing to take a young one. He went out to the ranch and felt a connection to this bay colt that was around two. He had brought him home, and he was the best horse he had ever had. He wasn't gonna let him go to just anyone.

I explained a little about Homestead and the animals. I told him that I really wanted another horse to spend time with Jolie. I then told Joe that, in all honesty, I was a bit overwhelmed, and I really could use some help. I told him that I would be honored if he entrusted Kodiak to me, and maybe he would consider coming and helping a day or two a week. It was the first time I saw a small smile on Joe's face. I then asked if I could meet Kodiak. I had a suspicion, but I needed to confirm it.

When we entered his barn, there was a large bay gelding that stood about seventeen hands high. He had a unique star and four white socks. I recognized him immediately. His registered name was

Kodiak Ursa because his star almost resembled the constellation Ursa Major. I did not let on that I remembered him and let Joe keep talking about all the things he and Kodiak had done. When he finished talking, I asked him if he would like to come out to Homestead and see the place for himself. I could see a glimmer in Joe's eyes. We decided they would come out the next morning around 9:00 a.m. I laughed and told Joe he knew the way. I told him to go back to the place it all started and take the second country lane past the farmhouse. They both looked at me for a moment, and then Joe started laughing.

"Damn, are you that kid that was working with Kodiak when I got him?"

I just smiled and said I could never forget Kodiak Ursa. Jerry finally caught up on the conversation when I said "them fellas" were my dad and my Uncle Bill. I think that was the time we all realized Kodiak would be coming home. Jerry walked me back to my Jeep and shook my hand. He said he did not know what to say. He thanked me for the way I spoke to his dad and how I made him feel needed. He said it felt like the first time he could breathe over the last few months. I told him I was happy to do it, and I was glad we would be able to keep Joe and Kodiak together. He shook my hand again, and I headed back to Homestead.

When I got back, I checked in on everyone and called Dad. I filled him in on Kodiak, and he said he would be at the cabin in the morning. I felt my anxiety rising, so I went to grab Jolie and Tapa and took a long walk. My peace has always been found in the quiet time when the world slows down around me.

Joe and Jerry arrived promptly at 9:00 a.m. Dad had come down earlier and brought one of his homemade coffee cakes. Julie was there and had already taken care of Dakotah as well as Pinky and Brain. I had Tapa and Jolie with us by the picnic table. I immediately noticed that Joe seemed to be struggling a little bit, so I got up to greet him. I introduce myself to him again and then introduced Julie, Dad, Jolie, and Tapa. It took a minute, and then I could see recognition coming back to him. He then smiled and asked if he could see where Kodiak would be staying. I planned on putting him next to

Jolie, so we headed over to the barn. I led Jolie back into her stall and left her with a sweet treat. Joe checked it all out, including the tack room, and then asked if he could bring Kodiak's tack out with him. I told him absolutely. I would not have my horse anywhere without my tack. I could see him relax a little, and then Dad stepped in to show him around a little more and give them time so they could reminisce about the past. Julie needed to head home, so I gave her a hug, and Jerry and I headed back to the picnic table. He said he noticed how quickly I picked up on the difference in Joe. I told him that it would not be a problem, and Joe would always have a place here at Homestead. Jerry was moving Joe on May 14, so he was hoping they could bring Kodiak out on the twelfth or thirteenth. We decided on the twelfth because I really did not want to do it on the thirteenth. I am not superstitious, but I did not want to take any chances by picking Friday the thirteenth.

In addition to the call from Jerry, I had received several messages from others who were interested in volunteering. Julie had also invited a few of her friends, and before I even realized it, we had become a family. Our youngest members were Julie and her friends, Mike and Amy. They were all seventeen and eighteen. Kelly was a single mom; her daughter was in school, and she was looking to volunteer. She really had no experience but was willing to do anything. Then we had Martin and Karen, a married couple with two teenagers at home. They were looking for an opportunity where they could volunteer together. Martin had been raised around cattle, and Karen had grown up with dogs and cats but loved all animals. Of course, Joe rounded out our family, bringing our total to ten, with Dad and Bill.

With the new additions to the family, I was able to find some time to spend up at the ranch. Fortunately, eight of the pregnant mares ended up with normal births, and we were still waiting on one. It was great having the time to lend a hand with all the extra horses.

I fell into a comfortable routine and was feeling optimistic about Homestead. Each morning I would get up early and take care of Tapa and Jolie. On the days Joe made it out, I made sure he got to feed Kodiak. Otherwise, I would feed him along with Jolie. Julie,

Mike, and Amy had taken on the care of Dakotah for most of the feedings and handled a large part of the mucking. They also seemed to love Pinky and Brain, so I left their feeding to the kids when they were there. There was always at least one of them around, but usually, it was two or all three. I asked them to keep an eye on Joe if I was not around, but I was surprised by how much they really seemed to enjoy their time with him. He had taught them how to groom Kodiak. They had taken that knowledge and began grooming Pinky and attempting to groom Brain when he allowed it. More than once I caught them gathered around Joe, and he was entertaining them with stories from his adventures.

Kelly made it out a couple of times a week and always kept the tack room and barn organized. She even planted some flowers and a small vegetable garden. She loved giving treats to the animals and was becoming more comfortable with them each day. Martin and Karen usually came out one day during the week and would come out with their boys on the weekend. At first, the boys were not too enthusiastic, but as they started to get more time with the animals, I noticed a lot less bickering and a lot more laughter. They loved Tapa, and she loved to wrestle with them in a way that reminded me of our first dog, Toby.

With the extra time, I found myself walking to the farmhouse when the weather permitted, usually with Jolie by my side. Tapa would sometime accompany us, but he had a sixth sense; and if someone were having a rough day, he would always find his way to their side. On these walks, I found myself telling Jolie all my innermost thoughts. I told her about my mom, about my time in the Army, and how I worried about how all this would play out. She heard my fears and my dreams and how angry I was about losing my leg. I told her things I had never told another human being. I resented not feeling whole. I hated that I would never ride again, and I wondered if I would ever find love. She was my therapist, silently listening as I got everything off my chest. I knew all my secrets were safe with her.

We would always stop to look at the mares with their foals before heading into the stables. I think she enjoyed seeing them as much as I did. I would place Jolie in the stable with some fresh water whenever we arrived. I knew I would be busy working for a while, and she seemed to enjoy visiting the mares through the back fence.

On one particularly rough day, when we entered, Jolie started pulling toward the tack room. I was not sure what she was after, but after a little pushing and shoving, she went into the stall. When I came back to get her after finishing up, she tried to pull me that way again. I thought maybe there was something in there, so I tied her up and went to check it out. I opened the door slowly and flipped the light on. I immediately watched a blurry ball of fur fly out the door. Cats are common around farms and barns. Although they aren't pets, like a dog or domesticated cat, they are usually friendly and tend to be excellent mousers. We always ended up giving them names and feeding them; although they tended to be a bit aloof. I did not recognize the ball of fur that shot past, and I had no idea how long it had been stuck in the tack room. I looked around to make sure there was not another one inside before I closed the door. Just before I closed the door, something else caught my eye. Sitting in the back corner on a saddle stand was my old saddle. A wave of nostalgia overtook me, and I ran my hand over the well-worn leather. It made me think back to what I had told Joe about my tack and how it would always be with my horse. It hit me kind of hard as I closed the door. I grabbed Jolie for our walk back. She tried to pull me toward the tack room again, but I assured her the cat was fine and probably finding something to eat. We took our time walking back in silence.

A few days later, when we arrived, Jolie once again tried to pull me to the tack room. I decided to let her have a look so she could see for herself the cat was no longer trapped. I opened the door, turned on the light, and allowed Jolie to stick her head in. She nickered and tossed her head. She pushed forward and laid her head on my old saddle. It probably still had my scent on it from the last time I was home before my injury. She pushed it with her muzzle, nearly knocking it off the stand. I finally backed her out and closed the door.

Dad came in about that time to check on the last pregnant mare. She was past the time we expected the birth, and he had called Cody to come out and check on her. I filled him in on the cat and how Jolie had been acting. He told me the cat's name was Lucy, and she had been hanging around a couple of months. He had been trying to catch her so Cody could spay her, but he might have to resort to a trap because she was quite a Houdini, getting in and out of all the other things he had tried.

When we were talking about Jolie, he asked if I had given any thought to riding again. I told him no; if I could not ride the way I used to, it just would not be the same. I loved the sense of freedom when I rode, and I could not do it anymore. What I did not tell him was how scared I was.

Cody arrived a few minutes later, and I went with him to check on the mare. She was one of the newer mares, and this was her first foal. Dad had asked about inducing the mare, and Cody told him that was really a last resort. It was not recommended, and he would keep an eye on her. By all accounts she was still fine, but we should probably set up a camera that we could monitor from our phones. Dad and Bill were old-school, but I told him I would take care of getting one up.

After running into town later that evening, I pulled into the stable to get the wireless camera up. It took a little longer than normal. I was not particularly good on ladders, but I was able to get it set up. Before I left, I stopped at the farmhouse so I could show Dad how to monitor it.

CHAPTER 10

Believing in Miracles

All seemed to be going well until a few days later. Jolie and I were walking to the farmhouse when I checked in on the mare. She was lying down, drenched in sweat, and was obviously in distress.

I immediately tried to call Dad, and it went to voice mail. I left a quick message and then tried Bill. After leaving another message, I remembered Dad telling me they were going to repair one of the outlying fences, and of course, there was no phone coverage. I put a call in to Cody but had to leave a message for him too. Jolie and I were too far away from the cabin to go back and get the Jeep, but we were still at least three miles from the farmhouse. I grabbed Jolie's lead and tried to run. I tripped and fell to the ground. I knew Jolie sensed my anxiety. I got up and grabbed her lead again. Jolie just stood there. I tugged on the lead rope, nearly in a panic. Jolie dropped to the ground. I was screaming in frustration, and she finally got up.

We took a few steps forward, and then she cut in front of me and dropped to the ground again. It was then it dawned on me; she did not go down like she was going to roll. She had tucked her front legs in and had then lowered her back. She was trying to tell me to get on. I had no idea what I was going to do, but I knew I had to trust her. I managed to figure out how to get on her once I took my leg off. I latched it under my belt and then grabbed a handful of her mane. She managed to get up without me falling off, and she started walking. I did not have the best balance on her, but she managed to get into a canter and then broke out in a full run. I was hanging on for dear life, but somehow, I was able to stay atop her.

As soon as we arrived at the stable, she dropped to the ground, and I slid from her back. I quickly put my leg on and entered the stable. I went straight for the young mare's stall. She was still lying down, and her foal was partially out, but she was struggling. I had helped birth foals in the past, so I calmly spoke to her and told her the next time she pushed, I would be pulling. Jolie was standing just outside the stall, watching. On the third try, the foal finally slid out. I immediately grabbed my pocketknife and cut the sack so I could clear the nose and mouth. At first, I thought I was too late; but as the mare reached around and started stimulating the foal, I saw it take its first breath. Just as the tears started falling from my eyes, I heard Cody's truck. I stepped back so he could look at both mom and baby. After checking both out, he stood and came over to me. He told me we had a brand-new filly and that both mom and baby seemed to be fine. He also told me that there could be complications since he had no idea how long the foal had been stuck, and we would just have to wait and see. Cody asked how I had managed to get there so quick, and I just told him that was a story for another day. I had not had time to process what had happened, and I certainly was not ready to talk about it. We stepped out of the stall, and I walked over to Jolie. I wrapped my arms around her neck and whispered a thank you.

Cody told me he had to leave, but he would stop back this evening. I put Jolie in a stall, where she could keep an eye on the new family, and I headed to the farmhouse. I took a shower and cleaned up. I tossed my clothes in the washing machine and grabbed a pair of sweats and a T-shirt from Dad. They were a little big, but they would work for now.

When I finally allowed myself to relax, it hit me. I collapsed as the realization I had ridden sank in. Not only had I ridden, I had ridden bareback. My phone rang as I was sitting there. It was Dad. They had just gotten cell coverage and got my message. I filled him in on what had happened with the mare and filly. He told me they were heading back and would see me shortly.

I headed back to the stable to check in on everyone. The mare was up walking around. The filly was standing but seemed to be somewhat shaky. I checked on Jolie and again thanked her for knowing what needed to be done. I sat and watched the mare, and she was not taking notice of the filly. I walked in to check on her to make sure she was producing milk, and everything seemed fine. I then went over to the filly to guide her to her mom in hopes she would start nursing. The filly seemed startled every time I touched her, and she was spending a lot of time smelling me. I finally maneuvered her under her mom, but the mare walked away. I waited for Dad and Bill to get back and thought, with some help, we might get her to nurse.

When they arrived, they came straight to the barn. It took three of us to tie down the mare and get the filly to take her first meal. When the filly stopped nursing, she backed away but stopped. We watched for a while, and whenever she moved, she seemed to be bumping into things. As soon as Cody returned, we filled him in on what had been happening. He first checked the mare, and she seemed to be fine. He then checked the filly. After a thorough exam, we tried to get her to nurse again. We had the same struggle as before but finally succeeded. After nursing, he observed the filly again. He turned to us and told us he could not be certain just yet, but the filly may be blind. If that was the case, and the mare continued to ignore the filly, we might have to switch over to bottle feeding using Foal-Lac. We decided to give it twenty-four hours before we made that decision.

I kept Jolie in the stall and borrowed Dad's truck to get back to the cabin. I checked in with everyone and told them what was happening at the ranch. Julie called her dad and asked if it would be okay to stay at the cabin tonight and take care of Tapa so I could go back to the ranch. He agreed, and I was so grateful for their willingness to help. He told Julie to let me know his wife had made dinner and for all of us not to worry. They were going to load it up and bring dinner out to Julie and drop off dinner for us at the farmhouse. I told Julie to thank him for all of us, and I headed into the cabin to grab some clothes so I could get back to the ranch.

Throughout the night I kept vigil in the stable. When it came to feed time, it continued to be a battle. Around 6:00 a.m. we finally decided to try a bottle. The filly didn't want to take it, so we called Cody. We were running out of options. When Cody arrived, we tried again. She still was refusing it. Jolie let out a whinny, and the filly raised her head in response. It was the first sign we witnessed of her communicating. Jolie repeated her whinny, and again the filly responded. I then had an idea. Actually, it was probably Jolie's idea, and I just understood it. I grabbed Jolie's lead rope and brought her over by the filly's stall door. I opened the door enough for Jolie to stand nearby. I took the bottle, and Jolie let out another whinny. The filly made a move toward her. After the next whinny, the filly was standing next to Jolie, almost leaning into her. I then took the bottle and offered it. The filly eagerly drank from the bottle. It was obvious to us the filly had found her new mom.

I kept Jolie at the stable for the first week. I was spending a lot of my time there anyway. I was so thankful for all the volunteers and how they all pitched in to cover what needed to be done at Homestead. At the end of the week, I was able to deliver some good news to them. We were bringing Jolie and the filly to Homestead, and they would all get to play a part in raising her. We decided to name her Miracle. Cody was still not certain about her eyesight, but other than that, she seemed to be doing extraordinarily well under the watchful eye of Jolie.

By the middle of June, everyone had fully fallen in love with Miracle. Cody had determined she was blind, but he believed she did see some shadows, so he was hopeful. Jolie was taking everything in stride. She spent part of her day with me, but we always made sure she was with Miracle during feeding time.

I moved my saddle and tack down to Homestead, but I still had not gotten the courage to ride. I knew I was capable, but I still had a mental block. Jolie never let me forget where my saddle was, and I knew her encouragement would help me break through.

We had also added a few new volunteers to our team as word got out about our menagerie of animals. As if two horses (Jolie and Kodiak), one filly (Miracle), two donkeys (Pinky and Brain), one calf

(Dakotah), and one very special dog (Tapa) wasn't enough, we were about to get the surprise of our life. Let us just say, there had never been a dull moment at Homestead, and we were about to welcome a few new residents that are going to turn this place upside down.

PART 3

Expect the Unexpected

CHAPTER 11

Celebration (One Pig Party)

With all the new interest, Homestead had become a very lively place. I started receiving e-mails and phone calls from people who wanted to come out and meet the animals. It was now summer, and it seemed parents were looking for ways to entertain the kids. In the past few weeks, we had started having people just show up unannounced. Thankfully, the new volunteers added a lot to our family. We were going to need it.

Ben was a contractor who had graciously offered to help fix up our smaller barn. We had nearly reached capacity in the main barn, and the smaller barn had not been used in years. He was going to rebuild the stalls and repair the broken barn door. Thankfully, Julie, Amy, and Mike were out of school, and they were going to help him and set up some additional fenced areas.

Lisa was a full-time IT person and was great at organizing. She loved the animals and started coming out on weekends. After some discussions about the influx of requests to visit, we decided we needed to figure out what hours we could be open to the public. She was willing to be there on weekends and would run point for visitors. We decided, for now, we would allow the public to come out on Saturday and Sunday, from 9:00 a.m. to 2:00 p.m.

Brad and Carla were the owners of the local newspaper. They were happy to come out and do whatever we needed, and they were also going to cover the expense of our signs and marketing. It was nice to see how the community had become involved.

We were quickly approaching the Fourth of July weekend, and after talking to Dad, we decided we would have a small celebration. We wanted to invite all the volunteers and their families out for a barbecue to thank them for everything thing they were doing. When we let everyone know, they decided to make it a potluck and pitch in on bringing food. Monday, July 4, I woke to a beautiful sunny day. After a quick bowl of cereal, I went out to check on everyone. This was a normal routine, and Tapa joyfully bounced along beside me. Everyone greeted us as we entered the barn.

Dakotah was growing quickly but behaved like a big puppy. The kids had been taking him for walks, and he easily followed them anywhere they wanted to go. The main property around the barn was completely fenced, so even if he happened to break away from them, he was not going to be loose. Jolie had Miracle tucked up next to her, with Kodiak remaining watchful in the next stall. During the day, we had been allowing the three of them to be together in the turnout pasture, and it was almost as if Kodiak had become the doting grand-father of Miracle. Pinky and Brain were in their combined stall area, huddled together. I always imagined them having the conversation about taking over the world. I had recently noticed one of the barn cats from up at the stable had been hanging around. I had started putting some cat food out for it, but I had not been able to get close enough to see if it was a boy or a girl. I started calling it Gizmo, as it reminded me of a little gremlin. I just hoped it never got wet and started acting like one. I looked around and thought what a perfect little world we had here at Homestead.

Julie arrived shortly afterward, and between us, we gave grain to all the animals. After we finished, she headed over to prepare Dakotah's bottle. We had introduced grain into his diet by sprinkling some of the powdered milk on it, but he still insisted on a bottle a couple of times a day. Everyone loved bottle feeding him, and he wanted it, so who was I to take away all the fun? She told me her folks would be out a little later to join the festivities.

I started preparing Miracle's bottle when Joe arrived with Jerry and his wife in tow. I asked Jerry if they wanted to give Miracle her bottle. I saw the spark of the little boy inside him. I explained to him how Jolie needed to be nearby and gave him the bottle. Joe stood over by Kodiak. He looked a little off today, but even on days like this, he never forgot Kodiak. I gave his shoulder a squeeze as I passed by.

Amy and Mike were the next to arrive. Amy's folks were divorced, but her mom was coming out later. Mike's two dads were also going to join us. Martin, Karen, their two boys, Zach and Mitchell, were coming, along with Kelly and her daughter. Lisa, Ben and his wife, and Brad and Carla rounded out the group. Cody was invited, but I was not sure if he and his new girlfriend would join us. Dad and Bill would be down when they finished up at the ranch. All in, we were looking at twenty-five to twenty-seven people. That was a lot of people for someone who was an only kid from a small family. I was excited, but I was also a little anxious. The next thing I realized, Tapa was by my side, and I was running my hand along his almost white fur.

It was a beautiful day, and with Ben's help, we had constructed several picnic tables. We decided the best place to eat was just outside the barn, in the grassy area. Dad, Bill, and I were doing the barbecuing. Dad had made homemade bread, Bill had concocted some sort of tropical fruit salad, I had made baked beans, and everyone else had brought so many side dishes we would be eating leftovers for a week. For dessert, we had several pies and a couple of cakes. We had planned on making some homemade ice cream a little later.

Everyone was laughing and having a great time. After everyone had eaten, we had set up a few games to play, but most everyone was happy just sitting around and talking. We really were one big family. Cody had arrived with his girlfriend, and everyone had been telling stories about growing up in Montana when my phone rang. Moments later, so did Dad's and Cody's phones. My call was from Danny. There had been an accident on Highway 2, and an entire truckload of feeder pigs had overturned, and the piglets where running everywhere. He was asking if we could help. Dad's and Cody's calls were regarding the same thing. When we told everyone what was happening, everyone headed for their cars. Kelly, Amy's mom, Jerry's wife, and Joe stayed behind to put away the food and take care of the animals.

When our caravan arrived at the accident site, it was chaos. First, we had to convince the state troopers to let us through; but as soon as Danny saw us, he gave the officer a thumb's up, and we were allowed to pass. What we estimated to be around two thousand piglets were running amuck. Dad had stopped to grab his horse trailer, I had the Jeep, and another empty trailer had just arrived. All you could see were people trying to grab and hold onto the piglets while getting them into one of the vehicles. It took us almost four hours before we finally reached a point where we thought we had all the pigs.

We pulled Dad's trailer and the Jeep over by the larger trailer and transferred the piglets into it. When it was loaded, they hooked up and headed out. We all looked at each other and began laughing. We were all filthy and exhausted, and I thought about what stories we all would be telling about our Fourth of July pig adventure. As we headed for our vehicles, I yelled out it was time for some pie and cake. We all deserved it. Just as Lisa was getting ready to enter her car, she heard something squealing. As she looked under her car, she found a little piglet, tucked behind one of her tires. She hollered for me, and as I approached, I saw her pull the little piglet out from underneath. She looked at me, and I looked at her. I just nodded, and she smiled. It looked like we were adding another resident to our menagerie at Homestead. I walked over to Cody to make sure he was coming back to the cabin and filled him in on the piglet. He told me there was no way he was missing out on a piece of apple pie, and he would check the piglet out when we got back.

As the parade of vehicles returned, we were met by the rest of the family. Once Lisa emerged with the piglet, all you could hear were the "oohs" and "ahhs." She set the piglet on the grass and noticed it was limping. When Cody arrived, he examined the piglet. It was a sow, and he estimated her to be about three to four weeks old. He believed she might have broken her leg, but he said there really was nothing he could do. It would be best to try to keep her still as much as possible. He told us to try to feed her the same milk replacement we were giving Dakotah.

We did not have any bottles small enough, so we tried placing some milk in a shallow bowl. We were thrilled when she was able to drink a little, and then we all giggled when we realized she had crawled into the bowl and had fallen asleep. I turned to Lisa and asked her what she would like to name her. She tried to decline, but I told her the same thing I had told Julie earlier: "You saved her. You have to name her." A little while later, she decided on the name Liberty. After all, it was the Fourth of July, and she did win her freedom.

We decided, for now, she would be kept in the cabin. She was so small, maybe five pounds. We took a large box to make her a bed and filled it with soft towels. Although it was July, Cody advised us to set up a heat lamp. He told us that she did not have other piglets to cuddle up with, so we should ideally maintain a temperature of around seventy-seven degrees. We checked the temperature with the heat lamp, and it was perfect. We set Liberty in the box while everyone got ready to leave. It had been an exciting and fun day, but everyone was ready to head home and clean up. Even with people taking leftovers home, I still had a refrigerator full of food.

When I woke the next morning, I went to check on Liberty. I found Tapa curled up next to the box, keeping a watchful eye on our new addition. When I opened the door, he headed out to take care of his business but came right back in. I guess he intended to stay by her side.

I mixed up a little milk and put it in a bowl. She drank every bit of it and went back to sleep. Tapa lay by her side while I went out to check on the other residents.

They all seemed to be as tired as I was. Of course, they had received so much attention and an unusual amount of treats yesterday, but they were still ready for their breakfast. Julie arrived first, with Martin and Karen showing up a few minutes later. The first question they all asked was, "How is Liberty?" I headed back to the cabin and picked up Liberty, tucking her into my shirt, like I used to do Tapa. She let out a little squeal and then nuzzled her nose into my neck. I had never felt a pig's nose before yesterday, and I was surprised by how rubbery they felt. Tapa and I headed out to the barn so everyone could see her for themselves.

Throughout the day, I think every volunteer made their way to Homestead. Lisa came by as soon as she had gotten off work. She had been researching how to raise a piglet on the internet, and we sat down to go over some ideas. I handed Liberty over to her, and I could see that Liberty was going to be one spoiled little pig. Okay, maybe not so little. We believed her to be a Yorkshire pig, and one of the things Lisa shared with me is that we could expect Liberty to weigh in somewhere between four hundred fifty to six hundred fifty pounds.

As the summer was coming to an end, it was time for Julie, Amy, and Mike to head back to school. Julie and Mike were seniors, and Amy was heading off to college. I was excited to know Amy was heading off to MSU but knew we would miss her. She assured us she would be back out whenever she was home.

Liberty continued living in the cabin, and she and Tapa were nearly inseparable. After finding a pig harness, she began making the morning rounds with us, and all the animals had become accustomed to her tagging along. Our biggest issue with her was her diet. No matter what we tried, she refused any type of pig feed. She loved fruits and vegetables, and she would eat human grains but refused the pig feed. We tried mixing it in with the fruits and vegetables, and she would eat everything but the pig feed. When we spoke to Cody, he was not overly concerned; but he did recommend some supplements, which we quickly added to her diet.

As we moved into fall, everyone seemed to be enjoying themselves. The weekends were exceptionally busy with visitors. Lisa had done a tremendous job of putting together an informational handout we could give to all the guests. It had the story of how Homestead Sanctuary started and a bio on each of the animals. Brad and Carla had created a beautiful sign for the entrance and took care of printing the handouts. Carla had also been helping me with grant applications to assist with all the expenses we had been incurring.

Liberty was growing, and it was almost time for her to move into a barn. We decided the small barn would be best for her. Ben oversaw building her an indoor/outdoor area, and Lisa was in charge of decorating. They both did an amazing job. Ben made sure she had a shaded area and a mud hole. He also reinforced the fence area to ensure she could not get out. Lisa decked out the perfect stall, fit for a princess. She decorated the walls, created a comfy bed, and even installed TV to keep her company. Ben had installed a heat system in the small barn similar to the main barn so she would be comfortable year-round. We did not want her to get lonely, so we decided to move Dakotah down with her. Of course, Julie and Mike had to decorate his area as well. We now had King Dakotah and Princess Liberty. We were turning into a royal family.

CHAPTER 12

Coping

As we were approaching September 11, my anxiety was running a little high. It was a day that had changed my life forever. Even though everything was going well, I just could not help it. One morning toward the end of August, while Jolie and I were on our morning walk to the ranch, a truck approached us on the main road. As it passed, the engine backfired, and I hit the ground. Jolie leaned her head down to make sure I was okay. It took several minutes before I could compose myself enough to get up. When we reached the ranch, I had calmed down, but there was something that seemed to be lurking in the shadows. That evening I had my first night terror. I was back in the Army, and I was reliving the worst parts. I woke drenched in sweat and my heart nearly beating out of my chest. Tapa was on the bed and laid his head upon my shoulder.

When I made it to the barn, the animals felt the tension in my body. Jolie noticed it the most, and her normal welcoming nicker had a different sound. It was the sound of concern. With no one around, it was easy to talk to the animals. I told them what had happened and tried to reassure them everything would be fine. When Jolie and I got ready to head to the ranch, she tried to nudge me toward the tack room, but my mind was elsewhere.

The night terrors continued for a week. I made an appointment with the VA, but it would take several weeks. I was already on some meds for my PTSD, but this was different. Finally, on the fourth or fifth day, I caught on to what Jolie was trying to tell me. Of course, it took her stepping in front of me, stopping me dead in my tracks, and then basically herding me back to the tack room before I understood what she was trying to tell me. As the saying goes, it was time to get back on the horse. I grabbed my tack and decided to saddle up Jolie. I did not tighten the cinch all the way, as I had no intention of getting on her yet. I wanted to see how the saddle would ride on her and how comfortable she would be. We walked to the ranch in silence, both of us lost in thought yet together. I took her to the riding arena, and we did some groundwork, more for my benefit than hers. I needed to do something to feel in control.

After a couple of days, I decided to try to ride. We had a mounting block, but after several failed attempts, I was getting frustrated. I tried with my leg on and with my leg off. I just could not figure it out. I know Jolie felt my frustration, and finally, she walked away from me and dropped down, just as she had done the first time. I went over to her and climbed into the saddle. She stood up, and there I was, sitting atop Jolie. I tucked my leg into the stirrup and tried to find my balance. I was so frustrated. This used to be second nature to me, but I tried to tell myself we would get there. I grabbed the reins, and we headed out for our first planned ride. We spent about an hour just walking, following some of the old trails I used to ride as a kid. It was different, yet it was the same. The next thing I knew, tears fell from my eyes.

When we returned to the farmhouse, I noticed Dad on the front porch, eating his lunch. As we approached, I saw him break out into a wide grin.

He looked me in the eyes and said, "About time."

He followed us over to the arena and watched as Jolie lowered us to the ground. He brought over my leg and asked how I taught her to do that. For the first time, I told him the whole story of what happened the day Miracle was born. He stood there in amazement and walked over to Jolie.

He looked into her eyes and said, "Thanks for giving me my kid back." I knew he was right. At least I was on my way.

We started riding every day. At first, we continued to walk, then trot, and then canter. I will not say it was easy, and I did take a few falls along the way; but other than my bruised ego, I was not hurt. Jolie continued to encourage me, and by mid-September I was riding with confidence again. As I found my peace, the night terrors went away. September 11 passed like any other day. I remembered what had happened and all the lives lost that day, but that shadow that had been lurking in my mind was gone.

CHAPTER 13

Building a Community

During this time, our weekend activity continued to grow. We had started getting requests from teachers to bring classes out for field trips. We needed to add a few volunteers if we were going to do this, and once again, we had some amazing people answer our request. Mandy and Matt were retired schoolteachers, and Cindy was a therapist. Lisa coordinated our field trips, and when she was available, she joined Mandy, Matt, and Cindy. The schoolkids absolutely loved coming out to Homestead, and we found that we could offer the visits around lunchtime, and the kids could bring sack lunches and eat at the picnic tables. Everyone had their favorite animal. Dakotah had his own calf halter, and Liberty had her own harness so they could join in the festivities while the kids ate their lunch.

I did receive an unusual request one afternoon. One of our schools reached out about bringing a group of special needs students out for a visit. The teacher said their abilities were varied, but they would be able to bring some additional help. I told her that I thought it would be fine, but I wanted to check with the volunteers that ran the program. When I approached Lisa, Mandy, Matt, and Cindy, they readily agreed to make it special. We coordinated with the teacher for September 30. Since it was a Friday, we decided on noon. They would eat their lunch when they arrived and then spend the afternoon with the animals. Afterward they would be ready to go home for the day.

When they arrived, we had everything decorated in bright colors. There was a total of nine kids, ranging from Down syndrome to various degrees of autism. The youngest looked to be about eight and the oldest fifteen or sixteen. Some of the kids' parents had come along to help, so we were able to keep plenty of eyes on all of them around the animals. When they finished their lunch, I noticed one girl paying attention to Liberty. I went over and found out she was there with her mom. Her mom told me her daughter's name was Kelsey, and she was autistic. She was nine years old and had been nonverbal for the past three years. She told me Kelsey loved animals and had two dogs at home.

I knelt by Kelsey and introduced myself. I asked her if she liked Liberty, and she nodded her head. I asked if she would like to pet her, and she broke into one of the biggest smiles I had ever seen. I walked over and grabbed Liberty's leash and brought her to meet Kelsey. I took Kelsey's hand and showed her how to pet Liberty and then gave her a treat to feed her. In a matter of minutes, Kelsey was down on the ground, and Liberty was cuddled up next to her. When everyone else went to meet the other animals in the barn, Kelsey wanted no part of it. I stayed behind with Kelsey and her mom. I asked Kelsey if she would like to see where Liberty lived. She nodded her head again, so I let her help hold the leash, and we walked over to the small barn. When we entered, Liberty went straight for her stall with Kelsey following her. They went over to Liberty's bed and promptly cuddled up. I asked her if she like Liberty's home, and she nodded again.

I stood there and talked to Kelsey's mom for a while and then noticed the time. We needed to head back up to the main barn and meet the others. Kelsey's mom told her it was time to go, and Kelsey shook her head no. She tried several more times, with Kelsey clinging tighter to Liberty. Finally, I went into the stall and sat down with them. I told Kelsey it was almost time for Liberty's dinner, and she would need dinner too. I explained that if she did what her mom wanted, they could come back anytime and see Liberty. She looked at me and then her mom. We both nodded, so Kelsey got up. What she did next shocked both her mom and me.

She leaned down and gave Liberty a big kiss, and then in almost a whisper, she said, "Bye, piggy."

It was garbled and hard to hear, but her mom and I both looked at her. Her mom spoke first and asked what she had said. In a little stronger voice, she repeated, "Bye, piggy." By this time, her mom had tears falling, and Kelsey looked confused. I reached down and picked her up and told her that it was okay, and her mom was simply happy. I told her she was Liberty's special friend, and she would have to come back soon. When we arrived back at the main barn, we told the teacher what had happened. She was as amazed as we were. The field trip was a success, with all the kids getting to cuddle Dakotah and give treats to the others. One of the students was legally blind, and he seemed to understand when he met Miracle. It might have been the first time he met an animal like him. The teacher was already talking about returning in the spring.

A few days later, I received an e-mail from the teacher. Kelsey's mom wanted to double-check and see if they really could come back out. I told her absolutely and to please give her my e-mail address and phone number. I received a call a little later in the day from Kelsey's mom. She was hoping to bring Kelsey and her husband out over the weekend. Kelsey had not spoken again, and she was hoping maybe she would around Liberty. I told them that would be perfect.

On Saturday when they arrived, I asked Lisa to text me. I met them at the cabin, and we walked back toward the small barn. I could tell Kelsey was excited. I asked if I could have a hug, and she ran into my arms. I asked her who we were going to see, and she looked up at me and said, "Piggy." I told her that was right, and I reminded her that the piggy's name was Liberty. I glanced over at her mom and dad. I can't remember ever seeing so much joy on someone's face. Over the next several months, Kelsey and her parents made many trips out to Homestead. It took a while, but Kelsey began vocalizing more often. She even learned to pronounce Liberty's name. To this day, they still come out and have become part of our Homestead family.

CHAPTER 14

Halloween Is for Kids (Literally)

The day before Halloween I received a call from Nate. He ran the dog and cat shelter in Kalispell. He told me that he had received a call from an anonymous person that two goats were being kept on a property just outside town, and the caller suspected they were going to be used for some type of ritual on Halloween. He had no idea who to contact or what to do. I reached out to Danny to fill him in. He was not sure what he could do, but he agreed to contact the owner.

When Danny called me back, he had spoken to the property owner and was told that the house was rented. He told Danny the renters were not authorized to have any animals on the property and gave Danny permission to go out and investigate. Danny asked for the police to accompany him on the visit since it was not clear why the goats were there or what they intended to do with them. When they arrived, they met three young men. Danny asked if they had goats on the property. They adamantly denied any animals on the property, and from what Danny told me, it was obvious they were lying. When the police officer informed them we had the owner's permission to look around, the young men slammed the door. The police officer radioed for backup and then went around to the back of the house. There was a small shed tucked away on the corner of the property. When the officer and Danny approached the shed, they could hear the goats inside. There was a chain and padlock on the door.

When the backup arrived, Danny grabbed a pair of bolt cutters and cut the padlock. When they opened the shed, they were greeted by two pair of eyes belonging to the goats, but they also found six black cats in a cage. When the police finally convinced the young men to come out of the house, they questioned them as to why they had the goats and the black cats. All three claimed to have no knowledge of the animals. With that, Danny stated that he would go ahead and take the animals until the "rightful" owners could be found. He then reached out to me, and in turn, I called Nate. I agreed to take the two goats, and Nate agreed to take the cats. A few hours later, Danny arrived with the goats. One was a pygmy coat, and one was a fainting goat. They were both adorable, but I had no idea what to do with goats. I called Ben and asked him to stop by when he had a chance so we could figure out what needed to be done. In the meantime, we put them in the main barn in one of the larger stalls. I sent an e-mail out to the volunteers, letting them know about our new addition. I set them up with feed, hay, and water, knowing we could deal with the rest the next day.

Halloween fell on a Monday, but as far out in the country as we were, we did not expect any kids trick-or-treating. Just in case, we had bought a few bags of candy for both the farmhouse and the cabin. Once again, I think most of the volunteers made it out sometime during the day to meet the new residents. Dad and Bill stopped by and affectionately kept calling each other an "old goat." They had said that to each other for years, but with the new additions, it kind of fit. Danny was asking around to see if anyone was missing goats, but for now, at least, they were safe.

Late afternoon I got a mysterious call. On the other end of the phone was a voice that obviously was disguised. I was told that "they" knew I had the goats, and they were planning on coming and taking them back. The person immediately hung up. I reached out to Danny and the police to update them on the call. We did not have much time to get a plan in place, so we had to work quickly. Danny immediately came out, and we brought Liberty into the cabin and took Dakotah back up to the main barn. The small barn was too secluded, and we did not want to take a risk with any of the animals.

Since we did not know how many were going to try to break in, the police wanted to protect it from the outside as well as the inside. We made sure all the animals were locked in their stalls with as much normalcy as possible under these conditions. The police set up a perimeter around the outskirts of the property. We set up the camera we had used when Liberty was born inside the barn. They placed two officers in the barn; Danny and I were told to stay in the cabin.

We sat quietly for several hours, watching the camera on my iPad. It had gotten dark and was eerily silent. I knew the officers were in place, but I was still concerned for all the animals. We did not have a police radio, so we had no idea what was happening. I know the officers had said they wanted to wait until they were inside the barn before trying to arrest them. They told me if they arrested them too soon, it would simply be trespassing, and they wanted to charge them with at least breaking and entering.

Suddenly I heard a loud commotion. There was a lot of yelling, and I could hear the animals carrying on. It seemed to go on forever, but I realized it was only a few minutes. When it quieted down, I immediately rushed out the door. I could tell in the dim lighting that the officers had four people in custody. As I approached, I recognized two of them from the home where we rescued the goats and cats. The other two were about the same age, but I did not remember seeing them before. I was wondering where the other guy was from the rented home but did not have time to stop and ask.

As I raced into the barn, I felt an officer grab me, and my heart fell to the floor. My only thought was something happened to one of the animals. As I turned around to look at him, he told me everything was fine. The officers around the perimeter saw them as they came out from the woods behind the cabin. They followed them, and as soon as they all entered the barn, the officers stepped out and announced they were under arrest. When they attempted to flee, the officers from the perimeter were waiting. There was a brief struggle, but no one was hurt. He told me, although they did not have any guns, they were loaded down with knives and ropes. I breathed a sigh of relief and then went inside to calm down the animals. Danny was right behind me and heard the entire story as well. He and I checked all the animals, and everyone was fine even though a little anxious. We closed the barn up and went back to talk to the officers. I did ask the officers about the third man from the house, but he said only the four they had in custody had come out of the woods. They were currently looking for the vehicle they had arrived in and could update me later. Once the officers had left, Danny loaded up his truck. I thanked him for coming out, and he just nodded. He told me he had to be there. He did not want anything to happen to Homestead. It was becoming a second home to him.

It was late, and I knew I needed to tell Dad what was going on. I was sure he had seen the police cruisers and had tried to call me several times. I had intentionally not told him about what was happening because I did not want him or Bill down here, but I guess it was time to face the music. As I started to call, I saw headlights coming down the drive. I could tell by the sound of the truck; I was too late. Dad was here, and this was going to be a long conversation. I walked over to truck as he got out. I told him everything was fine, and the animals were all safe. We walked into the cabin, and I explained everything that had happened. Dad proceeded to give me a lecture like only a dad could give. After he finished, I tried to explain why I had not called him. I told him I did not want him to worry and that I needed him to be safe. He looked me in the eyes and told me it was a father's job to always worry about his kids, no matter how old they were. He also said it was his job to keep me safe.

As the tears started to fall from his eyes, I realized this conversation was about much more than what had happened that night. He had kept all this bottled up inside him since the war and my injury. I reached over and took Dad in my arms and tried to reassure him that everything was going to be fine. I reminded him of what we had built and how lucky I was to have a place like this to call home. I told him how honored I was to have a dad that I knew would always love me and have my back. We visited for a little while longer, and he helped me move Dakotah and Liberty back to their barn. When he got ready to leave, he took another look around and told me how proud Mom would have been of me and how much she would love this place. I nodded and told him she was watching over both of us. I told him I loved him, and he said the same. We both knew it, but it was not something we said very often. Tonight it needed to be said.

The next morning, I received a call from the police. They had found the truck and trailer the group had intended to use about a mile away. I asked if the third guy from the house was the driver, and they told me no. They had gone to the house to check on him and brought him in for questioning. Come to find out, he had been the one to call Danny and me about what was happening. He knew the guys from college but had no idea they were capable of what they were planning. He didn't want anything to happen to the animals, so he had called us. I found out his name was Brian, and the officer I was speaking with told me he intended to call me later to thank me for saving the animals.

After I hung up, I went to the main barn to check in. Julie, Martin, and Karen were there and asked me if I had decided on names for our new additions. I smiled and told them yep. The Pygmy goat was Oscar, and the Fainting goat was BJ. I laughed and explained that the way Bill and Dad had carried on about each other being old goats, they deserved to be a couple of goats. Oscar was named for my dad, and BJ stood for Bill Junior. Bill was named after my grandpa. They all joined in my laughter and said they could not wait until Dad and Bill found out. I saddled up Jolie, and we headed up to the farmhouse. On the ride up I realized, not for the first time, how lucky I was to be surrounded by such beauty and wonderful people. But most of all, I was thankful for Jolie. I do not know if it was Mom, God, or something else that had brought us together, but whoever or whatever it was… I would forever be in their debt.

Later that day, I called Nate to fill him in and check on the cats. He was stunned by what had happened and told me, if Brian called, to pass along his thanks also. He said the cats were doing well and asked if it would be okay for him to bring his wife and kids out over the weekend. He had known of Homestead but had not been out to see it yet. I told him absolutely and to text me when they were on their way. I would meet them and show them around. They came out on Saturday. Nate was a tall guy, just over six feet, with dark, wavy hair. His wife, Connie, was maybe five feet with blond hair. They had two girls: one was ten and looked just like her dad; the other seven and looked like her mom. As we visited all the animals, the girls were telling me about all their pets. I had a feeling that Nate was a lot like me as a kid, bringing home every stray he found. Even today it seemed that the rescued dogs and cats had visiting privileges to his home.

The beginning of the next week, we started noticing some strange things going on in the main barn. On several mornings I came out to the barn to find various animals out of their stalls, wandering the barn. I was concerned the group that had tried to steal the goats was up to no good, so I called the police. They increased the patrols around the property, but there was no sign of anything missing or out of place. It was always just the animals. One morning Jolie was out; the next it was Kodiak. The following morning it was Pinky and Brain. One morning I found all the stall doors open, and all the animals were having their own party. Fortunately, we always kept the barn doors closed. I knew our volunteers were very conscientious about latching the stall doors, but even so, I sent a reminder out to everyone. I personally started checking the stalls before going to bed.

After a few days, I remembered I still had the camera up in the barn, so I went back to the recordings to see what was up. When I finally got a glimpse as to what was happening, I had to shake my head. It seemed BJ did not just stand for Bill Junior; it seemed he was the Best Jumper too. He was managing to jump up, on, and off the hay feeder in his stall and then out through the opening on the top of his stall door. There was a bench we had sitting outside the stall for the smaller kids to stand on so they could see. BJ was landing on the bench before jumping to the barn floor. He then would go over to one of the other stalls and had figured out how to raise the latch and slide it over. I watched the video in wonder. I had a feeling life with BJ was going to prove extremely interesting. In the meantime, we closed the upper part of the stall door. Mystery solved.

CHAPTER 15

Happy Holidays

Thanksgiving was quickly approaching, so Dad and I decided to do a Thanksgiving-style open house. The farmhouse was large, and many of the volunteers had never been up there or to the stables. We invited all the volunteers, Cody, Danny, Nate, and their families to stop by anytime. I was preparing a traditional Thanksgiving meal for Dad, Bill, and myself, and we would make sure there was plenty of food if anyone was still hungry when they got there. After the last big holiday get-together, we could only hope there would not be some type of an accident involving turkeys.

The regulars showed up to help take care of Homestead early that morning, and we would make sure we took care of the evening feed a little later. I used the Jeep to carry all the food up to the farmhouse, but I went back to Homestead to get Jolie and Tapa. With the number of people we were expecting, I needed these two nearby. As much as I loved all the extended family, I still was not used to large crowds.

Fortunately, Thanksgiving went off without a hitch. Dad figured we had close to forty people stop by. There were no major catastrophes except for a few spilled drinks. As Dad, Bill, and I sat on the front porch with a beer, we gave our thanks for the blessings we had in our lives and for each other.

Early December I received a call from Brian. I really hadn't expected him to call after all this time, but he told me he had been so embarrassed by what had happened. He had not gotten the nerve to call until now. We talked for about an hour, and I told him how thankful Nate and I were he at least called to warn us. I told him that we still had the goats and had named them Oscar and BJ and about BJ's adventure. Ben had built them their own play area where they could jump until their little hearts were content. Brian asked if he could come out and maybe see them one day. I found out he had been the one taking care of them and liked having them around. I told him he was welcome to come out anytime, and if he was interested, we were always looking for volunteers. He told me he had moved into his own apartment and would love to volunteer. He was off on Thursdays, so I told him to come out next Thursday, and I would show him around.

December was relatively quiet, and we had fewer visitors since it was cold and snowy. I loved this time of year. Everything was covered in a blanket of snow, and although it was too cold to go for long rides, Jolie and I still found time to take short rides around the cabin.

It was on one of these rides I got a look at her. I had heard her calls for the past week. She was an unusually large cow moose. Her calls were being made to attract a bull moose. I had not seen any moose on our property in years. I was happy to see her; although I knew how dangerous moose could be and was hoping she stayed out in the wooded area, away from the cabin.

As Christmas approached, the volunteers pitched in, and we decorated all kinds of pine trees. I think we had a total of fifteen trees at Homestead, plus three at the farmhouse, and one at Bill's. Bill told us he had a hell of a time getting all the sand out last year, so he stuck to a traditional one this year. We hosted a volunteer potluck Christmas party in the barn and had a small gift exchange. Dad dressed as Santa for the kids, and we gave each of the volunteers a special Homestead Sanctuary ornament we had handcrafted in Bozeman. At the end of the party, the volunteers gathered around and presented me with a beautiful saddle cross that had been made from Jolie's mane and tail hair. They told me it was a little thank you for allowing them to be part of Homestead. I thanked them and told them they were not just part of Homestead, they were Homestead.

Without them, there would not be a sanctuary for all the animals and the people that needed them. I told them I was excited to see what 2017 had in store for us, and as expected, we were going on another wild ride.

PART 4

Finding the Balance

CHAPTER 16

"Moose"letoe

January arrived with another snowstorm. On Wednesday, January 4, our high temperature was 3 degrees Fahrenheit and dropped to -22 degrees overnight. The regular volunteers remained faithful during these extremely snowy and cold temperatures, so I always kept hot coffee and tea set up at the cabin, along with a few healthy and maybe not-so-healthy snacks. I had come to realize that not only the animals depended on the volunteers but, to be honest, so did I. I knew that the work would get done with or without volunteers, but the bonds that were built between all of us had become the foundation of Homestead. I also realized all the preparation we completed before winter arrived was making things easier for all of us.

At the ranch, we always kept salt and mineral blocks on hand for our horses. I wanted to do the same at Homestead. We placed them in all the stalls and had even placed extra out along the tree line for our wildlife friends. For the past month or so, I had been keeping an eye on the blocks near the woods. I could tell they were being used by the deer and, I suspected, the moose. I noticed we had moose tracks getting closer and closer to the small barn. I frequently heard her calls out in the woods, but I never heard a response.

With the weather being so cold, I decided to bring Dakotah back up to the main barn and Liberty back up to the cabin. Ben had helped reinforce the fence around the backyard of the cabin before winter arrived. We had occasionally put Liberty out there for field trips, allowing the kids to interact with her up close and personal. It was a full house in the barn, and outside time was extremely limited, but having everyone in the main barn and cabin made me rest a little easier.

Just before winter set in, we finally were able to discover Gizmo was a girl when we had set a trap. After her spaying, she remained distant for a while; but when one of the volunteers, Patty, brought her a heated bed and tuna, she finally decided humans were not all bad. After Dakotah's move back to the main barn, she began following Tapa and me back to the cabin where she entertained us with her antics. Some mornings I would find Liberty, Tapa, and Gizmo all curled up together. One of my favorite pictures of them still hangs in the cabin today. Not often, if ever, would you find a pig, a dog, and a cat peacefully sleeping without a care in the world.

After moving Dakotah and Liberty, I decided to turn the heat off in the small barn and to leave one of the barn doors open just in case one of our wildlife friends needed a shelter. I left a heated water trough, a large mineral block, and some hay tucked away in a corner. Each morning I would take a walk to the small barn after finishing my morning chores. For the first week, I saw a few tracks but nothing else. I continued to make sure the water was not iced over, and there was hay. I decided to leave a couple stalls open with straw bedding. The second week I caught a glimpse of the moose by the small barn. When I checked later, I could tell she had been inside. I was glad I could provide some shelter for her during this bitter cold. I added some hay and grain and headed back to the cabin. This routine went on for a couple more weeks, but thankfully, she was gone by the time I got around to checking. By mid-February we had a little warm-up, and some of the snow had melted. I approached the barn just as she was exiting. The moment she saw me, she bolted for the woods. I was hoping I had not scared her off because I noticed she was pregnant. Moose typically deliver their babies around April or May, but she looked very pregnant, so I was concerned. For a couple of days, I saw no sign of her, but on the third day, I could tell she had returned.

The last week of February we had another major snowstorm. It snowed for four days without a break. I was unable to get out to the small barn for the first couple of days, but I knew I needed to check on it. On the third day I bundled up and set out as soon as it was daylight. I loaded up some grain and straw and strapped it to my back. The snow was so deep I could not use the gator to drive out there, so I started the slow trip on foot. I had a pair of old snowshoes, but with my leg, it was extremely difficult and slow. I was exhausted as the small barn finally came into view. I approached cautiously, and as I turned into the barn, I was confronted by a full-size moose. I was startled and fell backward. Moose can be overly aggressive, and in a brief moment, I thought of how stupid I was for not telling anyone I was coming out here. I think she was as startled as I was, and as I looked around, I realized not only was there one moose, she had also given birth to a pair of twins. Twins were not that rare in the moose world, but this was incredibly early for giving birth, and they were very tiny. Both were standing, so I took it as a good sign they were healthy. Trying not to make matters worse, I gently removed my pack and opened it. I brought out the hay and grain, placing it just inside the door. I scooted myself back out the door into the snow. It was cold, but I did not want to try to stand until I was farther way from the door. When I was finally able to stand, I was shaken. I gathered my thoughts and took a few deep breaths. I noticed the moose had not left the barn, so I was hoping she would stay put. I slowly made my way back to the cabin and nearly collapsed when I arrived. Tapa was by my side in an instant. I leaned down and buried my head and hands in his soft fur.

Suddenly I heard a crash coming from the kitchen. When I reached the door, I found a very guilty-looking Gizmo and equally guilty Liberty covered in flour. We had not only had a snowstorm outside; we apparently had one inside too. It seemed Gizmo had taken a liking to the flour canister and was encouraged, by a somewhat naughty pig, to push it off the counter and onto Liberty's back. My anger quickly subsided and turned into laughter. What a wonderful crazy life I was living.

After cleaning up the mess, I called Dad to tell him about the moose. He reminded me that moose could be dangerous, and they were wild animals. I told him I was not trying to make friends; I just wanted them to be safe. He did the dad talk, and I still knew I would go back out the next day with supplies.

On day four it was still snowing, but it had lessened considerably. I loaded up again and headed for the small barn. I approached cautiously and slowly entered. Mom moose and her twins were tucked back into the corner. Mom looked up but made no aggressive moves. She did stay between me and the twins, which was fine with me. I lowered my pack again and brought out more hay and grain. I spoke quietly to her and told her that her and her babies could stay as long as needed. I continued with this ritual each morning and asked all the volunteers to stay clear of the small barn. By the second week of March, it seemed that the weather was finally breaking; and as quickly as she had come, her and her twins were gone. I continued to check for a week, but there was no sign of her return. She had taken the twins and returned to the woods. I had never experienced such an intimate relationship with a wild animal, and although I knew she was going back where she belonged, I felt a little sad knowing I would never see her again.

CHAPTER 17

Highs and Lows

O n the upside, now that the weather was above freezing for most of the day, it was time to plan a celebration. Dakotah had turned a year old in February, and we decided to have a party at Homestead. We were going to make it open to the public, and the volunteers were taking care of decorations and food. Julie was so excited to show him off. Although he probably was close to one thousand pounds, he was so gentle and still acted like a big puppy. He had grown so accustomed to the horses; we could allow him in the same pasture with Kodiak and Jolie. He would have probably been fine with Miracle as well, but we did not want to take any chances. The party was planned for March 18. Brad and Carla handled all the marketing. They printed an article in their newspaper, along with some flyers inviting the public to come out and "cuddle a cow." They also printed a large birthday banner and signs. The other volunteers decorated and prepared the food. Everyone was excited to see the animals and each other after the long winter. Lisa had coordinated all the activities and the volunteers. The energy being generated was almost electrifying.

After saying hi to everyone and making the rounds, I headed over to the barn and saddled up Jolie. I did not want to spoil the day, but I needed some time to myself. I needed to ride out to the cemetery. Today was the day Mom had died. It had been sixteen years, but at times it seemed like only yesterday. I still spoke to her often, asking her advice or updating her on what was happening, but today I just needed to be there.

We rode out in silence. I did not need to tell Jolie anything; she already sensed my sadness. When I arrived, I noticed the fresh flowers on her grave. It was obvious Dad had already been there. I knew each year he rode out and sat there for sunrise and would return and watch the sunset with her. Jolie and I approached the gravesite, and she lowered herself so I could dismount. I walked over and sat down, remembering all the good times we had shared. I thought about things that had not crossed my mind in years. I thought about my Native American heritage and how she always told me to be proud of who I was.

I remembered when I started school how the kids would tease me. I did not look like the other kids, so I was an easy target. My dark hair and darker skin came from my mom, but my blue eyes were from my dad. I would come home, sometimes crying, and Mom would tell me stories about the Chippewa and how brave they were. I learned, by her example, how to embrace who I was and to stick up for myself and the underdogs. Dad taught me how to be strong in body, by Mom taught me how to be strong of mind. As I sat there, a two-tailed swallowtail butterfly landed on my arm. It was way too early in the season for a butterfly. I knew it was Mom, sending a message to me. I looked to the sky, thanking the Great Spirit for giving me my mom. I would continue my path, keeping true to the Chippewa belief that we share the earth with all animate and inanimate objects. I would always respect the earth and care for all objects as if they had a soul. With that, the butterfly took flight, and I watched until it flew out of sight. With this, Jolie approached and laid her head upon my shoulder. She was right; it was time to get back to the party. On the ride back, I once again experienced the joy I had felt as a child. Riding Jolie, we broke into a run; and although the cold stung my eyes to the point of tears, it was the rejuvenation I needed.

When I got back to Homestead, there were cars and trucks parked everywhere. I arrived back at the barn to find it full of people. I decided to go to the cabin first so I could take Jolie's saddle off and properly care for her. When we got to the cabin, the backyard was filled with people talking excitedly and taking pictures with Liberty. Tapa was out back, enjoying all the attention as well. I went around front and dismounted. It was there I found Kelsey with her mom and dad. Kelsey was excited to see me and ran into my arms. I picked her up, and she was beaming. I asked her if she had seen Liberty yet, and she told me, in a full sentence, "I saw Liberty, and I got a picture." I looked to her mom and dad, and they told me she had been doing so much better; and although she would always have challenges, she was learning new coping and communication skills. In my mind, all I could think of was her first visit here and the tiny pig who changed her world. I asked if they wanted to come inside for a bit, but they declined. They had been there for a while and were hoping they would have a chance to see me. They were just getting ready to head home when I arrived. I gave Kelsey another hug and told her to be good. I then headed back to Jolie and finished getting her ready to go back to the barn.

I went inside to use the bathroom before taking Jolie back, and then I saw Gizmo, sitting atop the refrigerator. She looked me straight in the eye and proceeded to push off the six pack of beer I had sitting up there. I could not move quick enough to catch any of them, and they shattered when they hit the ground. I looked back up at her and could tell immediately she was upset about being left in the cabin while the party was going on outside. I opened the back door for her and then cleaned up the mess. I certainly knew where I fell in this pecking order, and it was somewhere behind a cat.

After returning Jolie to her stall, I made the rounds, meeting a lot of new people and saying thank you to everyone who had come out. I caught up with Lisa, and she told me she had several checks for me, and I could expect some calls this next week regarding other donations. I thanked her again for everything she was doing and then caught Julie and Dakotah out of the corner of my eye. They were surrounded by people. As I made my way over, I could see a line nearly wrapped around the side of the barn. Apparently, everyone did want to "cuddle a cow," and Dakotah was just eating up all the attention and all the extra treats.

As the sun started to set, things finally started to wind down. Everyone was busy cleaning up, but there were still a few people wandering around. A little later, I noticed an older car coming up the drive while everyone else pulled away. I saw a mom and dad get out of the car with a small boy in tow. He was maybe five or six. I could hear them telling him that the place was closed, and they would have to come back another time. The little boy was crying, saying he wanted to see the cow. As they turned to go back to their car, I stopped them. I introduced myself and knelt by the little boy.

I asked him his name, and he replied, "Aaron."

I looked up at his mom and dad and then back down to him.

I said, "How about one quick look at the cow before you leave?"

He looked to his mom and dad, and they nodded their head. I reached out my hand, and we walked over to the barn. Dakotah was already back in his stall, so I picked Aaron up and brought him into the stall with me. We walked over to Dakotah, who raised his head. Aaron reached down and petted Dakotah and then leaned in for a big hug. I looked up just in time to see his mom take a picture with her phone. We stayed with Dakotah a few minutes, and then Aaron's mom and dad said it was time for them to leave. He needed a bath and get to bed. We walked out of the stall, and I set Aaron down. I told him he would have to come back and meet all the animals. He again looked to his mom and dad, and they nodded. I thought about a story Mom had told me when I was about Aaron's age. As I walked them to their car, I asked Aaron to look up and find his star. He looked up and then looked back at me.

I asked him, "Do you not know about your star?" He shook his head, so I picked him up and pointed to the sky. "You see that bright star right over there?" as I pointed to the sky. He nodded.

I told him that was his star, and everybody had their own star. I pointed out his mommy's star and his daddy's star. I told him how his star always kept a watchful eye over him when he was awake. I also let him know that his star could not sleep until he did. I put him down and told him he should hurry home, get his bath, and then go to sleep because his star needed to sleep too. As I sat him down, he grabbed his dad's hand and told his dad to hurry up, they needed to get home. His mom and dad turned to me and whispered their thanks. At least that night there would be no problem getting Aaron to bed.

As we finished cleaning up and the volunteers finally made their way to their own cars, I could honestly say that was the largest gathering we had ever had on the property. I was drained, both physically and mentally, but I was excited about what the year had in store for Homestead. I reached the cabin, making sure Tapa, Liberty, and Gizmo were safely tucked inside and headed for a long-overdue, hot shower. This party would go down in the Homestead history as one of the greatest parties ever thrown.

CHAPTER 18

Community/Family

The next morning, I looked at the checks and donations that had come in from the party. Lisa was right. We had received a lot of money, almost $8,000. The community had really shown up and supported Homestead. I reached out to Brad and Carla and asked if they could write a thank you on Homestead's behalf and put it in the paper. They were excited to help and said they would get something out with the next issue. Lisa was also right about receiving some phone calls. It was more than just a few. We were able to add another six people to our volunteer family, and we had several businesses who were offering their support.

One of the biggest surprises was when I received a call from the ranch supply store where we bought all the supplies and grain for the ranch and Homestead. Sam, the owner of the store, had reached out to Purina and told them about Homestead. He told me that Purina and his store would be covering the cost of all the grain we needed at Homestead for at least the next year. He needed me to stop by the next time I was in town, and we would fill out all the necessary paperwork; and whenever we needed something, all I needed to do was call and place the order. They would deliver it to us. What an amazing gift.

As we moved into April, we were busier than ever. We had school field trips planned for at least twice a week through the end of the school year. Several of the new volunteers were retired and helped during the week. They loved helping when the kids came.

The volunteer family was a mix of older and young, men and women, those with money and those who were barely scraping by to pay the bills. The funny thing was, it all worked. No major issues, and everyone got along. They were there for one reason only—the animals.

At the ranch, we had been busy planting the fields with alfalfa hay. We relied on at least three cuts a year to keep our horses in hay through the winter. With the extra animals at Homestead, we wanted to seed an additional fifty acres. Fortunately, things were going so well I could spend more of my time helping at the ranch. Of course, that meant I got to drive the tractor. I remember the first time I got to drive a tractor. I must have been nine or ten. I thought I was so cool, sitting up in the cab, helping with the planting. Looking back, I realized what a magical childhood I had been given. I was glad I was in a position now to share some of my experiences with the kids of Montana.

CHAPTER 19

Confronting the Past

On May 4 I was scheduled for a variety of medical tests down at Fort Harrison Medical Center. I had been putting it off for the past six months, but I knew I needed to go. My prosthetic needed adjustment, and I knew I still needed to talk to someone about my anxiety. I had been doing better, thanks to Homestead; but as the day approached, I was getting anxious again. I caught myself spending more and more time with Jolie and Tapa, the two of them helping me to find my peace. I nearly canceled the appointment, but when I mentioned it to Dad, he refused to let me do that and instead insisted on taking me.

On the drive down, Dad tried to talk, but I was stuck in my own head. I was imagining what they would find wrong—maybe something wrong with my leg or, worse, something wrong with my head. I had been having nightmares again, not the night terrors like before but nightmares about what I had experienced, only somehow distorted. When we arrived, I went to check in. My medical evaluation was first. They did blood work, took X-rays, and a complete physical exam. I was relieved when I finally saw Dr. Kim, and he said everything looked good. He told me they would call when the blood work results were back. He sent me over to the prosthetic's technician where she made a few adjustments to my leg. The next part was what I had been dreading.

I headed over to mental health to meet Dr. Jenkins. Before I arrived, I had broken out in a sweat. When I sat down with him, I was not sure what to say. Dr. Jenkins seemed close to my age and did not look like a doctor. He reminded me more of someone I would probably be friends with and have a beer. He asked a few questions, but when he asked about my sleep, I lied and said I was sleeping fine. He looked at me and told me if I could not be honest with him, he would not be able to help me. He could tell by looking at me I was not fine at all. After what seemed like an hour, but what I realized later was only minutes, I started to open up and tell him about the anxiety and nightmares. He reassured me that I was not alone, and both veterans and civilians suffering from PTSD often had trouble with both anxiety and sleep. He suggested I join a veteran support group in Kalispell. He went ahead and renewed my prescriptions and wanted me to follow up with him in six months. When I walked out, I felt a little better. I promised him I would check out the support group he mentioned.

When I caught up with Dad, he asked how I was doing. I told him honestly I was not sure. Physically, I was doing well. Mentally, I was going to work on it. On the drive back, I began telling Dad about some of the nightmares. It was the first time we had really discussed what he had experienced and what I had gone through. He had never really talked about his time in the military, and I certainly had not. On the way home, we stopped at Moose's Saloon for pizza and a beer. By the time Dad dropped me off at home, I was feeling a lot better. As I walked into the cabin, I saw a pair of shiny eyes over on the end table. This was followed by a crash. The lamp from the table was sitting on the floor, and Gizmo glared at me from the end table. Oops, she was telling me I forgot to leave a light on. I picked up the lamp and headed for the kitchen. This called for some tuna. Gizmo forgave me eventually, but I was learning I had to be a better cat parent, or else I had to make sure I did not leave anything breakable within a paw's swipe.

The next morning, I called the Vet Center and found they had a group of post-911 veterans that met every other week. The next meeting was on May 16, so I added it to my Google calendar. I figured I would check it out. What could it hurt?

CHAPTER 20

When New and Old Collide

T he volunteers were once again planning a birthday party, this time for Miracle. It was hard to believe she would be turning one. I thought back to that day and everything that happened. The party was scheduled for May 27. We were going to celebrate Miracle's birthday and Memorial Day. Lisa was, once again, coordinating everything. She would make sure we had plenty of food and volunteers to cover the crowd. Brad and Carla were taking care of marketing. Carla also suggested we reach out to the Montana School for the Deaf and Blind in Kalispell and do something special. I called the school a little later in the day and spoke to Cheryl, one of the administrators. She had heard of Homestead but had not had a chance to stop by. I told her about Miracle and how she was thriving even though she was blind. We decided it was best for her to see Homestead in person, so we set up a visit for Thursday afternoon.

When Cheryl arrived, I took her on a tour. She was genuinely excited and had some great ideas on how we could partner with the school. She told me the visually impaired students could make braille books with all the animals' bios that the students could use when they visited. She said they would also provide us copies to keep at Homestead. She also suggested her hearing-impaired students could make signs using ASL for the names of the animals that we could post alongside the regular nameplates and bios. This would be a great way for her students to contribute. I was in awe of how quickly she looked for a way to help Homestead. When I originally reached out, I was hoping to set up a field trip or two for the students and do something for them. She assured me that making her students part of the Homestead community would mean so much more to them; it would be nice to be included. We decided she would get her students working on the projects and would have the signs to me by May 23 so we could get them posted before the field trip on May 25. I reached out to Lisa to let her know about the school's field trip on the twenty-fifth, and she agreed to take the day off from her other job to help coordinate. That week was going to be extremely busy, but I was confident we could do it.

With the warmer weather, I wanted to utilize the small barn again. After cleaning it out thoroughly, I had taken Liberty back down to her palace. Dakotah had been doing so well with the horses I decided to keep him in the main barn, and we moved BJ and Oscar to the small barn. BJ and Oscar were happy playing with Liberty, so we converted the area surrounding the small barn into a large outdoor space where they could play. I am not sure who loved the mud bog more, Liberty or the goats.

When the sixteenth rolled around, I nearly talked myself out of going to the meeting at the Vet Center. I always felt weird around people I did not know, and I had no idea what to expect. I took a long ride in the morning with Jolie and told her about my fear. I still don't know how she does it, but I could feel her reassuring me. I knew she wanted me to go. When we got back, I decided I would go, but I would take Tapa with me. If dogs were not allowed, I would have an excuse to leave.

When I arrived at the Vet Center, I was directed to a large recreational room. As soon as I walked in, I was approached by a guy named Chris. He reached out and shook my hand. He was a Marine and led the meeting. I introduced myself and Tapa. As I looked around, I saw a variety of people. There were about twelve people total, some men and some women. A few had obvious physical injuries, and a few others had support dogs. The room was set up with a circle of chairs. People had brought snacks and had set them along the table in the back. When Chris got ready to start, he asked everyone to have a seat.

A welcoming face motioned me over and pointed to the seat next to her. I found out her name was Shannon, and she was Air Force. I introduced myself and Tapa just as Chris started to speak. He welcomed everyone and then took a minute to introduce me. I was thankful he did not make me stand up and tell people about myself. I would have no idea what to say. Instead he went around the circle and have everyone introduce themselves, branch of service, and where they served. After that, he had a couple of topics he wanted to discuss. The first was discussing the paperwork and steps needed if filing for disability. The other was regarding an assignment he had given two weeks before. Apparently, he had asked everyone to try one thing that was out of their comfort zone. As people spoke, some of them were funny, like going to the bathroom while out in public. Others were more serious. Mac, another soldier, said he went to the store by himself.

When it got to me, I said the first thing that came to my mind, "I showed up to this meeting."

That answer was met with a few giggles but mostly a lot of nods. After that, Chris opened the floor to anyone. A few people spoke about various things going on in their lives. Some mentioned other programs they attended to help with PTSD. When the meeting was finished, people hung around to socialize. Shannon introduced me to Mac and David. We stood there, talking for a while. Mac had suffered a traumatic brain injury and had just started coming to the meetings about a month ago. David was a former medic and was suffering from PTSD. Shannon was injured in Afghanistan and had recently been diagnosed with PTSD. I introduced them all to Tapa and showed them my leg. It was nice to be talking to people that really understood some of the things I had been feeling. They asked me what I was doing now, and I told them about Homestead. They all seemed interested, so I gave them my phone number and invited them out to see it for themselves. I think David was the most surprised when I told him I was riding again. He grew up with horses but had not been around them in years. I again encouraged them to come and visit as I said goodbye. As I drove back home, I knew I would be back.

As promised, Cheryl delivered the signs from her students, and we quickly got them mounted next to the nameplates. At the entrance to the barn, we set out some brochures she provided regarding American Sign Language. She also brought me an advanced copy of the braille book. I was intrigued by the grouping of dots and their meaning. I was excited about the students' visit on Thursday.

Lisa had reorganized our normal field-trip agenda to accommodate the students that were coming, and Cheryl assured me they would have extra staff on hand as well. They arrived in two buses. The students ranged from five to twenty-one years of age. Cheryl had organized them by age groups and abilities. Each group was assigned two teachers and two volunteers. Some other volunteers were assigned as animal handlers. I took care of Miracle and Jolie.

As the students were finishing their lunches, I brought Miracle and Jolie out from the barn. I introduced Miracle and told them we were celebrating her first birthday. The school had assigned a sign-language interpreter for groups with deaf students, so they signed while I spoke. To my surprise, every student pulled out a homemade birthday card for Miracle. I thanked each of them as they brought me their cards. I made sure each of the students had the opportunity to pet her and give her a treat. I made sure to give a good description of Miracle when the visually impaired students came up. As each group finished with Miracle, they went with the various volunteers to visit the other animals.

In the last group there was a boy, about thirteen, who was blind. When he came up to meet Miracle, I could tell it was all new to him. I asked him if he had ever met a horse before. He responded no and told me he had recently moved here from St. Louis. As I guided his hand to pet Miracle, I could feel him taking in every muscle and curve of her body. She responded with a nicker to his touch. He asked several more questions about her, including what she ate and how she became blind. I think the one that touched me the most though was when he asked me if a blind person could ride a horse. I assured him that many blind people rode, some competitively. Before he walked away, I asked him his name. He told me his name was Jordan.

After the groups dispersed, Cheryl came up. She told me how much the students had enjoyed working on the projects for Homestead, and she hoped we could do more together in the fall. I told her I would really like that. I asked her about Jordan. She told me he was fourteen, and he had recently moved to Montana to live with his grandparents. His mom and dad had been killed in a car accident. I only thought about it for a moment before asking Cheryl to pass along my name and phone number to his grandparents. She told me she would, and then I went to put Miracle in her stall. I then saddled Jolie. When the students finished with all the animals, they gathered at the picnic tables next to the big barn. There was one more thing I wanted to show them. When they all quieted down, I rolled up my pant leg and removed my prosthetic. I heard a few surprised reactions, one of them I recognized as Cheryl's. Jolie lay down, and I got on. In mere seconds I was sitting atop her in my saddle and slowly walked her over to the students. I told them they should never let anyone tell them what they can or cannot do.

I explained, a year ago I thought I would never ride again, but I had a horse that never gave up on me. I told each of them I would not give up on them either, and I was expecting great things from them. Jolie and I started off with a walk then trot then canter. I could tell the teachers were explaining to the visually impaired students what was happening. When we finished, I dismounted. I put my leg back on, and we walked over to the students. I was specifically looking for Jordan. As I looked at his face, I could tell his teacher had done a great job of explaining things to him because he had a grin from ear to ear. As the students loaded up, Lisa reminded them we were having Miracle's party on Saturday, and there would be cake and ice cream. I was hoping at least some of them would be back with their parents over the weekend. Lisa and I went back over to the homemade birthday cards, and we decided to do a large collage so we could put it up for Saturday. Lisa asked Cathy, another volunteer, if she would help, and off the two of them went to figure it out.

Miracle's party was another huge success. Lisa and the volunteers had done it again. I recognized many of the students who had been out for field trips, including some from the deaf-and-blind school. I was a little disappointed that I had not seen Jordan, and I still hoped his grandparents would call. Other faces were familiar too. I knew it was not their first trip to Homestead. Amy was back from college and had picked up with Julie and Mike as if she had not been away. Danny stopped by, and so did Cody. Jerry and his wife brought Joe out early so I could take him for a ride.

I saddled Jolie and Kodiak, and as we rode, Joe talked a lot about when Jerry was young. I think it was the happiest I had ever seen him. There had been a steady flow of people all day, and by dusk, we were cleaning up. Dad and Bill stopped but did not stick around. I knew, like me, they did not care for large groups of people. Lisa was the last to leave, and I pulled her aside and asked if she would like a beer. She was grateful, so I grabbed a couple from the cabin, and we began checking all the stall doors and barns. As we walked, I thanked her again for everything she had been doing for Homestead. She just nodded and told me how much she enjoyed it. I told her, if we were ever able to hire someone, I wanted it to be her. I did not know if it would ever happen, but I needed her to know the thought had crossed my mind. She told me we could cross that bridge if we ever got to it. We finished our beers just as we finished checking the barns. Everyone was accounted for, safe and sound. I said goodbye to Lisa and headed for the cabin. Tapa and Gizmo were already tucked inside.

CHAPTER 21

When Heroes Fall

It was mid-June when I was able to return to the Vet Center for a meeting. When I arrived, I was met by Chris, Shannon, and David. I asked about Mac, but no one had talked to him. I had taken Tapa with me again, and he stayed glued to my side. I was telling them about Miracle and her birthday party, and apparently, several other vets had tuned in on our conversation. When Chris called the meeting to order, he asked if I would tell everyone about Homestead. I had not planned on it, but somehow, I managed to not only tell them about Homestead but about Jolie and how she had enabled me to ride again. There were a lot of questions, and by the time the meeting ended, the next meeting had been scheduled to take place at Homestead. When I got ready to leave, I asked Shannon if she had Mac's number. She did, and she gave it to me.

I waited until Wednesday morning to give Mac a call. The first call went to voice mail, so I waited a while and then followed up with a text. It was late afternoon when I got a call back. I could tell, by Mac's voice, something was wrong. He was obviously drunk, but there was something else in his voice. I did not want to pry; I know how I felt when I came home. I did tell him that we were having the next meeting at Homestead, and I hoped he could make it. My next call was to Chris. I told him about my conversation with Mac, and he promised to check in on him.

Dad and I decided to have another Fourth of July barbecue for the volunteers as a way of saying thank you. Since the fourth fell on a Tuesday, we decided to have the party on Sunday, the second. Along with the volunteers and their families, we invited Danny, Cody, Nate, Sam, Cheryl, and Chris from the Vet Center. We also had invited the people who had "adopted" one of the animals online and were giving monthly donations for their care. Even though the party was for the volunteers, they insisted on decorating and bringing side dishes. A few asked about bringing fireworks, but I explained that we never had any fireworks other than a few sparklers because we did not want to scare any of the animals.

As the volunteers were planning for the Fourth of July, I was planning on the Vet Center meeting that I was hosting on June 27. I asked Ben and Lisa to help. Ben was former military, and Lisa could help me pull it off. We decided to let Chris kick off the meeting, and when he was finished, we would all be available to take people around to meet the animals.

The morning of the twenty-seventh was beautiful. I was feeling very anxious, so I went for a ride. Jolie always sensed my mental state, and she set off at a slow pace so I could lose myself in thought. We had been riding more often, and she knew her way on most of the trails without my guidance. As my mind wandered, I kept coming back to two questions. The first was, why was I so nervous about having this group out to Homestead? The second was, is there a way for Homestead to help others, just as it had me? When we got back, I was more relaxed but still didn't have any answers.

Chris was the first to arrive. I met him, and we walked over to the big barn. He looked around and was immediately drawn to Dakotah. I handed Chris a treat to feed him. As Dakotah took the treat, he rolled his big tongue over Chris's hand. Chris let out a genuine laugh and thanked me for hosting the meeting. I told him how happy, but anxious, I was about having the group out. When he asked me why, I shrugged my shoulders. Shannon and David arrived next. David took one look at Kodiak, and I knew he was hooked. The rest of the group started showing up, and I looked around for Mac. He had not made it. I asked Chris if he had spoken to him, and he told me he had. He shared with me that one of Mac's buddies had committed suicide, and he was not doing well.

Just as we were about to start the meeting, a Ford 150 pulled up. It was Mac. As he got out of his truck, I walked over to meet him. I told him thanks for coming. He said he almost did not, and if it had been at the Vet Center, he would not have come. We walked over and sat down as Chris started the meeting. After thanking everyone for coming out and thanking me for hosting, he began talking. He asked how many of us knew a veteran that had committed suicide. Almost everyone's hand went up. He then asked how many of us had thought about it. Slowly the hands began to raise. I looked over at Mac, and his hand was in the air. Chris was great at leading the group through this tough conversation. He brought up the feelings of hopelessness, of being lost back in this world, and the ghosts that haunted all of us. We talked for almost two hours. When we were finished, he told everyone that Homestead Sanctuary was a place of healing, and it was time to meet the animals. Lisa and Ben had brought Liberty up from the small barn, and everyone broke out in laughter as they saw her dressed in a red-white-and-blue tutu with a cowboy hat placed on her head. Lisa told them Liberty needed to try out her Fourth of July outfit. That was all it took to break the tension in the air. Shannon immediately headed for Liberty, as did several of the others. As everyone made their way around the main barn, I could tell Chris was right; this was a place of healing.

As I looked to find Mac, I saw Gizmo weaving in and out around his legs. He would occasionally bend down to pet her. She had become social, but I had never seen her behave like that. I walked over and asked Mac if he wanted a beer. He said that would be great, so we headed for the cabin. I grabbed the beers, and we sat out front. He asked some questions, all the while Gizmo kept weaving in and out of his legs. I guess at one point we must have been engaged in our conversation and had set our beers on the table. I was too slow to realize what was happening when Gizmo jumped on the table and immediately shoved Mac's beer into his lap. For a minute, I was not sure how Mac was going to react, but then he reached down and picked the bottle up and at the same time offered his lap to Gizmo.

I looked at him and told him I was sorry; she was not happy when she was being ignored. He laughed, and I went to get him a towel. I think I knew right then; Gizmo was not going to be staying with me for long. It took another three months and several visits from Mac before she decided to jump in his truck when he got ready to leave. She refused to get out, and Mac just smiled. I told him it looked like he had himself a cat, and he nodded.

I realized after everyone left that I had been nervous for no reason at all. I had enjoyed having them out, and Chris had asked about future meetings. I told him if the weather was nice, maybe we could do once a month. I also had another idea, but I wanted to talk to Dad first.

CHAPTER 22

The Longest Week Ever

The Fourth of July weekend was extremely busy. We had decided to be closed to the public on Sunday so everyone could enjoy the party, but we would be open on Monday and the fourth so there would be plenty of time for people to come out and visit. Somehow the volunteers had managed to get Pinky and Brain in red-white-and-blue straw hats as well Liberty in her tutu. The entire weekend was filled with fun and laughter. The volunteer party ended up with about sixty people, and again, there were enough leftovers to feed everyone for a week.

By Wednesday evening, I was worn out after the past week's activities. After checking on all the animals for the night, I took a quick shower and headed for bed. Sometime after midnight, I was unceremoniously dumped from my bed onto the floor. It took me a minute or two to figure out what had happened. When the first aftershock hit, I knew there had been an earthquake. As soon as it subsided, I grabbed my clothes and phone. I checked on Gizmo and found her under the couch, and Tapa was by my side. Fortunately, I only had a couple of cabinet doors open with a few cans on the floor. Living with Gizmo had taught me to keep everything put away. I grabbed Tapa's leash, which I never used around Homestead, and took her with me to check on everyone. Before we reached the barn, there was another aftershock. It was hard to see in the dark, but everyone in the big barn appeared to be fine. There were a few items tossed around in the barn but nothing I needed to deal with right then. We headed to the small barn to check on Liberty, BJ, and Oscar. To my relief, they were okay and just seemed a little anxious.

I gave Dad a call, and he answered immediately. He was fine and had already heard from Bill. He was on his way over to the stables. Bill was heading out to the east pasture where several of our mares were grazing. I told him Tapa and I would head to the west pasture where the geldings and stallion were kept. Fortunately, I had equipped the wrangler with a light bar and spotlight. When Tapa and I arrived, we could tell the front fence of the pasture was fine. I opened the gate and drove through. I decided to drive the fence line first. I preferred to check it on horseback, but it was too dark. I would come back later with Jolie to check it out properly.

As I made my way around the fence, I found a couple of boards down, nothing that would allow the horses to get out. I nailed the boards back into place and kept moving. Finally, as I approached the southwest corner of the pasture, I found the bachelor herd. I turned off the engine and used a flashlight to approach them. They all appeared to be healthy and unaffected as another trimmer shook the ground. It was not severe, and the horses did not react, so I headed back to the Jeep. After checking the remaining fence, I gave Dad a call. He told me the stables were good, and Bill had checked in and reported no issues. It seemed we were lucky, and everyone and everything was fine. I told Dad I would be out with Jolie after daybreak to check the fence line thoroughly.

Just as I arrived back at the cabin, my phone rang. It was Danny. He wanted to check in and make sure everyone was okay. He was on his way over to Route 93. There was a section of power lines down, and he was called in to help divert traffic. I told him I would be happy to lend a hand, so he gave me directions to a section north of Kalispell. I jumped in the Wrangler and headed out. I sent Dad a text and let him know where I was going. As I turned onto 93, I could clearly see where the power was out. I had already put my light bar on and went ahead and switched on my spotlight. I caught up with Danny about ten miles out of town. I pulled over to the side of the road and hit my flashers. I found out, about another two miles up the road, the earthquake had caused a pole with power lines to topple over onto the highway. The crew was already on their way to make a temporary repair, but we needed to stop all traffic until they arrived.

As Danny was bringing me up to speed, a Dodge Charger flew past us. Danny and I both said, "shit," and jumped in the Wrangler. We heard it before we saw it. There was a loud crash, and we knew the car had hit the pole. Fortunately, the police were already on site. The car had hit the pole and bounced away from it. The electrical lines were not touching it, so we could get to them. I grabbed my fire extinguisher and broke out in a run. Danny called 911 and requested an ambulance. After what seemed like forever, the officers were able to get the door open. Inside were two teenagers trapped by their seatbelts. When the ambulance arrived and they were able to extricate the teens, they found a dog in the back seat. When they carried it out, I could tell it was seriously hurt. I grabbed my phone and called Cody. He told me to meet him at his clinic in Kalispell. I let Danny know where I was going. He told me to be careful and good luck.

With it being the early morning hours, I made it to the clinic in record time. Cody was just pulling in. I grabbed the pup and headed for the door. I carried it straight to the exam room while Cody washed up. While Cody examined the pup, I was able to get a good look. The pup was a young male and looked to be a boxer-bulldog mix. I heard Cody on the phone, talking to one of his techs. He asked he tech to come in. The pup was in bad shape and needed surgery. I stayed around until the tech arrived and asked Cody to call me when he could. I drove back to Homestead, thinking about the kids and dog.

When I got back, I started on the morning chores. There was no way I could sleep. As I was finishing up the morning feed, my phone rang again. It was Danny. He had just left the accident site, and the power pole had been moved off the road. He told me the police informed him that the kids were banged up, but nothing too serious. He asked about the dog, and I told him I was waiting to hear from Cody.

Dad stopped by shortly after I spoke to Danny. He asked how things had gone, and I told him about the accident. He told me to not worry about the fence line; he and Bill would get to it. He wanted me to get some rest and would check in on me later. Late morning Cody finally called. He told me he wasn't sure the dog would make it, but he had done everything he could. He told me, along with all the cuts, the dog had a broken leg and had broken his back. He said if he did survive, he would probably be paralyzed. I was shaken but wanted the dog's family to know.

I drove to the hospital and found the kids' parents in the waiting area. I introduced myself and asked how the kids were doing. Just as Danny had said, no serious injuries. One had a broken wrist, but other than that, it was all bumps and bruises. I told them I had taken the dog to the vet and filled them in on his condition. I was not expecting their reaction. I was hoping their reaction was a result of worrying about their kids, but I was fairly sure I was wrong. I was told, in no uncertain terms, that they did not care about the "damn" dog, and I should have just left it to die. They told me to do whatever I wanted to do with the dog; they were not paying for any vet bills. I reassured them I was not worried about the bills. I just wanted to make sure the kids knew about their dog. I left there baffled and more than a little disappointed. On my way out, I did ask about the dog's name. They told me his name was Rebel. I called Cody to update him. He told me not to worry about it; we would sort it all out later.

It was over a week before I heard from Cody. Rebel was doing much better, but as expected, he was paralyzed. Cody also told me he had spoken to the parents, and they had given him the same response. He told me he could call Nate at the rescue and see if he could take him. I did not want Rebel going to a rescue, even if it was a genuinely nice one. He needed space to recover. I told Cody that as soon as Rebel was ready to leave, I wanted to bring him to Homestead. I did not know the first thing about caring for a paralyzed dog, but I knew I needed to figure it out. I reached out to Nate and told him what had happened. He told me he would get with Cody and figure out what he would need. He also asked if Rebel had bladder and bowel control. I told him I had no idea, so he told me he would find out.

When I returned to Homestead, I began thinking about what needed to be done to accommodate a paralyzed pup. I knew of paralyzed dogs that had a type of wheelchair. I looked at the cabin to see what we would need to change. There were two steps into the cabin. I knew Ben would be able to build a ramp, and we could figure out the rest.

It was another week before Cody and Nate brought Rebel to Homestead. Rebel was healing well, and Nate had a dog wheelchair that fit him for now. I brought Tapa outside so he could meet Rebel. Tapa approached Rebel first, and as dog's do, they sniffed each other. There were no growls or sudden moves. Tapa smelled the wheels and then went back to Rebel's head. Rebel dropped down on his front paws, and so did Tapa. Then Tapa bounced, and so did Rebel. The next thing I realized, I had two dogs playing in the front yard. I smiled, knowing it would all be fine. Cody told me Rebel did have bowel and bladder control, but I would need to keep him on a regular schedule. Paralyzed pups were known for getting infections, so we would have to keep an eye on him and have regular checkups. When Cody and Nate left, I ushered the boys into the cabin. As we entered, I heard a crash from the kitchen. It was time for Rebel to meet Gizmo.

The remaining part of the summer was relatively quiet, and thankfully, Rebel settled in very well. Several of the volunteers offered to help with Rebel when I was busy, and we had again found ourselves in a nice routine. I took time to relish the peacefulness because I knew in my mind the fall would bring some big changes. I just had not realized how big.

PART 5

Keeping Balance

CHAPTER 23

The Horse Project

After discussing my plan with Dad and getting his agreement, I reached out to Chris. I explained that I wanted to start a program to work with veterans and partner them with horses from the ranch. I told him that it would be more than just teaching them to ride. I wanted them to bond with a horse. Jolie was my inspiration. I could talk to her and tell her anything. I wanted others to have the same opportunity. He thought it would be a great idea, and he would spread the word. I told him initially I would like no more than six or eight participants. We would be meeting at the ranch. It took Chris a month or so to get the approvals and participants, so our first meeting was on August 30. I wanted to make sure to have the program started before the holiday and September 11. I know these were a couple of my PTSD triggers, and I suspected they were for others.

I was waiting anxiously for the arrival of our initial group on Wednesday. Dad and I had brought ten of the ranch horses to the arena along with Kodiak and Jolie. We had each horse tied up with a nameplate and a little write-up about them. I had asked Joe about using Kodiak, and he was thrilled that Kodiak would get to participate. David was one of the first to arrive, and his eyes lit up when he saw Kodiak. The others arrived shortly afterward. In total, there were eight: six men and two women.

As we made our way to the stable, I explained what I had in mind. I wanted them to not only learn about horses but make the horse part of them. While telling them a little about Jolie and my experience, I explained and demonstrated the basics about being around horses, such as never walk behind a horse, approach from the side, and how to use a lead rope. I then asked them to go around and meet the horses. I asked them to meet several of the horses and see if there was a connection then decide on the one they wanted to work with over the next several months. I laid my hand on Jolie and watched as they began engaging with the horses. To no surprise, David went straight to Kodiak and stood by his side, lead rope in hand. I watched several others meet a few and then return to one which called to them. In one case, a young mare chose her companion by reaching out and pulling the young man to her. He smiled and grabbed her lead rope.

Twenty minutes later, each person was matched to a horse. I think they were surprised by what I told them next. I asked each of them to take the lead rope as I opened the arena gates. Dad would take the extra horses back to the stables as I led the way to one of our larger pastures. I told them it was time for them to take their horse for a walk. I wanted them to spend some time getting to know their horses. I was a little amused by their reactions, but they all started walking away with their horse. I stayed with Jolie, taking a walk of our own, observing the interactions. When I gathered everyone back together, it had been almost an hour. As we walked back to the arena, I noticed a difference in the energy surrounding the group. In my heart, I knew this was going to work.

When we arrived at the arena, I showed each of them the proper way to tie up and spent the next thirty minutes reviewing the parts of horse and having everyone use their hands to explore their own horse. It was getting late, so I told them Dad and I would put the horses away today, but beginning next week, they would be responsible for bringing their horse to the arena and taking them back to their stall. I was not surprised when several offered to stay and help.

I had originally planned for this to be once a week for six weeks, but within the first few weeks, I noticed two things. First, several of the participants were coming out more than once a week, which was fine by me. The other was, six weeks was not enough. We were covering the basics for the first few weeks: feed, putting on a halter, care, grooming, and some basic groundwork. By week four, we lost a couple of participants, but the six that remained were fully engaged, and I could see a change in their mannerisms. We then went on to bridles, bits, and then finally, the proper way to saddle a horse. We did not have enough saddles in the beginning, but when word got out about what we were doing, we had several people donate saddles that they no longer needed.

By the end of week six, it was time to start working on riding. Dad and I had specifically picked horses that had a gentle demeanor and were familiar with having a rider on their back. Dad and Bill were both helping by this time so we could spend more individual time with the riders. The group was evenly split between those that had ridden and those that had not. We ended up spending the next four weeks working in the arena, then pastures, and finally, the trails we had on the property. A few of the riders had begun asking if they could buy their horses. As we were approaching week ten, I knew the program was coming to an end. I had mixed emotions. I had watched people and horses transform but was apprehensive about what would happen next.

Dad, Bill, and I sat on the farmhouse porch, having a beer following one of the sessions. We talked about what we were going to do next. Obviously, those that had a place to take their horses could certainly buy them, but what about the others? Bill suggested we might want to consider turning his barn into a boarding facility. I had not thought about his place in a long time. He had his horse out there, but his barn was large and had eight nice-size stalls. We had occasionally used the space when we were overstocked at the ranch. He had a fence around eighty acres, and we could share several of the pastures. Bill would need some extra help, but the income brought in by boarding would offset the cost of someone part-time.

At the final meeting, we were ready, and so were the participants. When David arrived, he came up and laid a hand on my shoulder. He thanked me for everything. His relationship with Kodiak was remarkable. It was not like Joe's, but it was strong in its own way. He was thrilled that Kodiak was part of Homestead, so he would continue to get to see him. When the others arrived, I had them gather around with their horses. I told them how proud I was of them and all that they had accomplished over the past ten weeks. I also told them they would always be welcome at the ranch and at Homestead. Finally, I explained if they were interested in their horse, we had come up with a couple of options. Of course, if they had a place for a horse and wanted to buy, we would certainly agree to selling. I also informed them we would be opening a boarding facility out at Bill's place. If they wanted to buy their horse and board them out at Bill's, they get first option of open stalls. By the end of November, two had taken their horses home, and the other three were comfortably residing out at Bill's. David was hired as part-time help and would then stop by Homestead to check on Kodiak. I had spoken to Chris, and with the success of this program, we would have another in the spring. He told me several people had already expressed an interest, so we planned on a group of ten to twelve.

CHAPTER 24

Just a Trim

Back at Homestead, we were preparing for another winter. Social media and word of mouth kept us busy. Dakotah and Liberty were as spoiled as ever. Both had taken a liking to watermelon, and it was not unusual to pull up and find several melons sitting on the porch of the cabin. Liberty had grown into quite the big girl, but she was still a favorite with all the kids that came to visit. BJ had only gotten out a few times—that we know of.

Once, when we were mowing behind their stalls in the outdoor area, he decided the mower was a great place to jump onto to jump over the fence. We were not sure about the others. We should have named him Houdini. Oscar, on the other hand, was very calm and enjoying life. Tapa had taken Rebel under his wing and was showing him everything he could do. I would take the boys outside first thing in the morning. After their breakfast, I would get Rebel on his wheels, and they would make the morning rounds with me. If I had to leave, one of the wonderful volunteers would make sure Rebel was back in the cabin by noon. As we learned about dogs with special needs, we found they should not spend all their time on their wheels. He was happy taking a nap until I got home. In the evening, the three of us would again check on all the animals and usually spend time hanging out in the front yard.

In October, when Cody was out for one of his regular checks of the animals, he mentioned Liberty would need her hooves trimmed.

I am sure I had a stupid look on my face when he said it. I knew that the horses, donkeys, etc., all had to have foot care, but a pig? I then thought about Dakotah and asked him about cattle. He smiled and said every animal needed hoof and/or paw care. I thanked him and gave our farrier a call. He was scheduled to come out before winter to take care of the horses, but I needed to fill him in on Homestead and all the animals. When he returned my call, he said he would be out the following Tuesday. He asked if any of the animals would need to be tranquillized. I assured him they were all very gentle and would not be a problem.

When he arrived Tuesday afternoon, after taking care of the horses at the ranch, we went to the main barn at Homestead. Jolie and Kodiak were used to the process. Even Pinky and Brain were okay with a little coaxing. When we got to Dakotah, it was obvious he did not want any part of the activities. With all hands-on deck, we finally were able to coral him in his stall, and we were able to clean and trim his hooves. We thought the worst was over. Boy, were we wrong. When we arrived at the small barn, he checked BJ and Oscar and told us they were fine for another six months. And then there was Liberty. I will tell you now what we had not known then: pigs do not like being picked up! In fact, that is the understatement of the year. Here is the commentary that should have accompanied our adventure.

> The players enter the stall. Odds are stacked in the human favor. Three grown adults-one pig.
>
> Pig approaches Player 1 and receives a pat on the head and an apple piece.
>
> Player 2 approaches as Player 1 grabs pig around middle.
>
> Player 2 grabs pig around back.
>
> Players 1 and 2 attempts to lift pig.

Pig makes a twisting move while rendering a squeal loud enough to be heard in the next county.

Players 1 and 2 are startled, drop pig, and fall, covering their ears from the offending sound.

Pig escapes, and Players 1 and 2 are now seated on the floor.

Player 3, previously blocking escape to outside pen, reaches for pig.

Pig fakes left, then right, and bolts through the door, between Player 3's legs. *Score!*

Pig 1, Humans 0.

Humans regather and grab pig harness, proceed to outdoor arena.

Pig is now near mud bog. Player 3 approaches with harness.

Pig responds and allows Player 3 to place harness.

Player 1 approaches with lead rope.

As Player 1 attempts to engage lead rope, pig reverses course into mud bog, dragging Player 3 with her.

Player 1 lunges for pig and misses.

Player 1 and Player 3 now sitting in mud bog while pig makes a quick run for it.

Player 2, now armed with more apple slices, obtains lead rope from Player 1 and approaches pig.

Player 2 engages lead rope while feeding pig and stands to accept congratulations.

Pig sees Players 1 and 3 approach, covered in mud, and makes a break for it, dragging Player 2 to the ground.

With a quick move, pig breaks between Player 1 and 3, dragging Player 2 into the mud bog. *Score!* Pig 2, Humans 0.

Players 1 and 3 jumped to grab pig and miss, finding themselves in mud bog.

Pig emerges from mud bog, dragging lead rope and proceeds to take a bow, running to the far side of the outdoor arena.

Audience's laughter has grown to epic proportions.

Farrier proceeds to truck to obtain tranquilizer.

A sweet treat later, and pig is peacefully resting. Hoof trimming complete.

When we all managed to pry ourselves out of the mud, we were laughing. Another volunteer took the tranquilizer in a piece of watermelon out to Liberty and led her back to her stall. We took a hose and attempted to rinse off some of the mud. I hadn't laughed that hard in a long time. It felt good.

CHAPTER 25

Holiday Magic

As the holidays approached, we had a few special field trips coming to Homestead. Montana children's regional medical facility was planning an outing for several children and their families, and the deaf-and-blind school were scheduled to return. Everyone worked extra hard in making sure we could provide a wonderful experience for both groups. I had spoken to Cheryl about a project for the kids at the deaf-and-blind school, and we decided on ornaments for a Christmas tree. We had a fifty-foot pine at the entrance to Homestead, and I had always wanted to decorate it. My thoughts were, we could make it into a community Christmas tree this year. I asked if Jordan was still attending the school, and she told me yes, but he was struggling. I asked for more information, but she told me that was all she could say.

Lisa and several of the volunteers pitched in and brought ornaments for all the kids to decorate. Dad and I bought all the lights for the tree and had them in place before the Thanksgiving open house. The families from the medical center seemed to enjoy their day at Homestead. For many of the kids and their siblings, this was the first "nonhospital" activity they had done in a long time. There were a lot of pictures and laughter. I believe the animals understood the difference between this field trip and others we had hosted. They were calm; even BJ spent time entertaining them with his "fainting" routine. Before they left, we took each of their ornaments and placed them on the tree. That night I thought about the kids and how much they were going through. I was proud to be able to deliver a little bit of "normalcy" to their lives.

Just before Thanksgiving, the deaf-and-blind school returned. I recognized many of the students. They brought handmade ornaments for the tree, and then they each made an additional ornament while visiting. They were excited about seeing the animals again and had updated the nameplates and bios if needed. This time I introduced each of them to Rebel. I told them his story and what an important part he played here at Homestead. As they all came forward and said hello to Rebel, I noticed Jordan hanging back. When I finished, I walked over to him and asked how he was doing. He said he was fine, but I could tell in his voice that was not the case. I asked him if he wanted to walk with me over to check on Miracle and Jolie, and I got to see a glimmer of the kid I remembered. As we walked, I asked what he had been up to all summer.

He just shrugged his shoulders and said, "Nothing."

I said, certainly, he must have done something fun, and he told me no. His grandparents did not let him do anything. As we visited, he said his grandparents were nice, but they never let him hang out with friends or go anywhere. When I asked him why, he told me he thought it was because he was blind. It was like they were so afraid of him getting hurt he never got to be a kid. He said coming out to Homestead was one of the best days he could remember and why he was so excited about coming back. I had him enter the stall with me when we got to the barn. First, we went to Jolie, and she playfully pushed at his shoulder. He leaned into her, and I could tell he was relaxing. When we went over to Miracle, he told me he could not believe how much she had grown. I smiled, knowing since he was unable to judged her by sight, he had to do it by feel. He was right; she was really growing fast. We joined the rest of the group a little later and took all the ornaments down to the tree. Even with the two field trips, we had only covered a ridiculously small portion.

The following morning, I reached out to Brad and Carla and asked about placing a full-page ad in the paper, asking the community to help us decorate the tree. I told them that I wanted people to bring a special ornament out for the tree and a note explaining its meaning. Ben had built two large boards where people could place the messages, safe from the weather and where others could read them. Brad and Carla said they would take care of it and make some flyers to post in the local businesses in town. I also called Cheryl and told her about my conversation with Jordan. For whatever reason, I just could not seem to get him out of my mind. I asked again if she had passed my messages along to his grandparents and if she could think of anything I could do to help. She assured me she had spoken to the grandparents twice, and both times they told her they would call. I asked if she thought it would do any good if I told Jordan I wanted to speak to them. She was not so sure that was a good idea but did not know what else to try. She said she would talk to Jordan later that day.

Thanksgiving was another wonderful time with my Homestead family. As expected, everyone ate too much, but it was fun being surrounded by family and friends. Jolie, Tapa, and Rebel were all at the farmhouse, and I think they enjoyed the extra attention. David even went back to the cabin and rode Kodiak over to the farmhouse when Joe asked him. Dad and Bill were having a great time, and Bill said having young people out to his place to take care of the boarded horses was keeping him young. I think he just enjoyed the extra company.

I was a little surprised when my phone rang later that evening. It was Jordan. He told me he had tried to talk to his grandparents, but they would not listen and wouldn't call me. I found out he had left the house, and he was calling to say goodbye. He said he was taking the bus back to St. Louis. I asked him not to leave yet, I would be right there. I asked Dad to take care of the animals, and I headed for the Jeep. As soon as I was on the road, I called Cheryl. When she answered, I told her what was going on and asked if she could call Jordan's grandparents. She agreed and told me she would call me back. I headed for the bus station to find Jordan.

He was easy to spot; not many travelers on Thanksgiving Day. As I approached, I heard him say, "Hi, Alex." I asked how he knew it was me, and he said everyone has a distinctive walk. Mine was easy to hear because of my leg. He was a smart kid; I was in over my head.

We sat and talked for a while. He had it all planned out. He had been talking to a buddy back in St. Louis whose parents agreed he could stay if his grandparents agreed. He had a girl from school pretend to be his grandma on the phone, and apparently, the family bought it. I asked him if living in Montana was so bad. He told me no. He liked the school a lot and had made friends. The problem was his grandparents treated him like he could not do anything for himself, and he felt like a prisoner in their house. I asked if he had told his grandparents that, and he said he tried several times, but they just would not listen. He had only called me because I had been so nice to him, and he really did enjoy coming out to Homestead. He wanted to say goodbye in person but had no way to get out to Homestead, so he had to call instead. Before long, I saw Cheryl enter the bus station with an elderly couple. Jordan just sat there and asked me why I had called them. I told him that I had called them because he was only fifteen, and I did not want him making a big mistake.

As the elderly couple approached, I could feel the tension in Jordan building. When they arrived, they immediately started hammering him with questions. I stood up with my arm protectively around Jordan and politely asked them to calm down. They both looked at me, and I took the opportunity to introduce myself to them. I told them Jordan had called me to say goodbye, but what I was hoping for was that we could all go somewhere and talk. At first, they told me it was none of my business, but after a few minutes, they agreed. With it being Thanksgiving, nothing was open, so I asked if they would all come out to the farmhouse with me. They agreed, and Cheryl drove the grandparents while Jordan rode with me. He was quiet at first but then told me thanks.

When we got to the farmhouse, almost everyone was gone. Dad and Bill were cleaning up with the help of Lisa. I grabbed some lemonade, and we all headed to the porch. We must have talked for a couple of hours. I tried to moderate the discussion between Jordan and his grandparents. It turns out that part of the reason they were being overprotective of Jordan was they had already lost their daughter and could not think about losing him. Both Cheryl and I assured them Jordan was a good kid with a good head on his shoulders. We all said, in front of him, he was a teenager and was going to make mistakes, but he needed to have some freedom. By the end of the conversation, they agreed to allow Cheryl to find them a family counselor and that every Saturday Jordan could come and help at Homestead. If for any reason they could not bring him, I would go and pick him up.

Over the next few weeks, the tree transformed into a beautiful Christmas tree. Every evening we would walk down to the tree and read the new notes about the ornaments. Some were funny, some sad. Many were remembering a loved one or a loved pet. Some were homemade, and some were store bought. The one thing that shone through was the love people had and that they were willing to share that love with Homestead.

It was on one of these walks, back toward the cabin, that I heard her. It was in the distance, but I would recognize that moose call anywhere. The next morning, I called Ben. I explained that the moose was back. I needed to find a way to put up a shelter by the tree line. There was no way to move everyone into the main barn this year, but I really wanted her to have somewhere to go. Ben said he would not have time to build something, but he knew a guy who had some prefab buildings, and we might be able to get one delivered. If so, he could install what we needed on the inside. I asked him to check into it and let me know.

Ben called back later that evening. His buddy agreed to deliver us a used prefab building that had been used as a garage for farm equipment. The building already had electric run in it, but it would need a few repairs. Ben said he offered to give it to Homestead, and he was certain his team could do whatever repairs would be needed to make it safe for the winter.

On Saturday a large flatbed with the building arrived. A crane had been dropped off on Friday and was already waiting near the tree line. Ben and his crew had been out during the week to prepare a level spot for the building. The building reminded me of a large Quonset hut with sliding doors on both ends. We watched in amazement as the crane raised and then lowered the building onto the land. I had Jordan by my side and described to him everything that was happening.

By the end of Sunday, Ben had once again created an amazing space for the animals. He had quickly repaired both sliding doors and had built a brace that would allow us to only keep one door partially open for the animals. He had constructed a large, open area inside with two stalls to one side. He also created a room where we could keep grain and tools locked up. On the other side, he had created a separate area for storing hay so we could a avoid having to carry it all winter. Ben's electrician had come out and run electric to the building from the small barn. He had also installed a few lights as well as a few outlets. We carried a large water trough into the building, away from the door, and loaded a water tank on the gator so we could fill it. We would not be able to run water to the building before spring, so we would still have to carry it this winter. After a few trips from the main barn to the hut, we had loaded grain, hay, and straw. We had placed straw in the two stalls as well as the open area and put a heater in the water trough and plugged it in. The grain was locked up for now, and if we saw the moose, we would put some out for her. As we finished up, I thanked everyone for helping. I was sure many of them thought I was insane, but at least they cared enough to go along with my crazy ideas.

Within a week we began seeing signs of her, and it appeared her twins were still by her side. There were multiple tracks, some smaller than the others. One evening, while sitting on the porch, I heard her call again. It was closer than before. I decided to walk toward the hut. The sun was setting, and I came to a stop about one hundred feet from the hut's entrance. I stood silently as she emerged from the woods. She looked up, and I swear she looked directly into my eyes. It was only a moment, but in that moment there was a connection. She turned back and let out another call. Out of the woods, two smaller images emerged. The family of three moved quietly into the hut. I stood there silently for a few minutes before moving back toward the cabin. Tomorrow would be soon enough to put the grain down. Tonight we all needed our rest.

Christmas was a wonderful family gathering. All the houses and barns were decorated along with the most beautiful community tree. It seemed most of Western Montana had heard of Homestead, and I ended up being interviewed by several newspapers and even appeared on TV. That was something I really was not comfortable doing, but they agreed to come to Homestead to film and would focus on the animals instead of me. For Christmas dinner, we were keeping it to a small group. Lisa and David were coming over, along with Jordan and his grandparents. Bill, Dad, and I were happy to keep this a small gathering where we could give thanks for everything that had happened and the blessings that had been bestowed on us. That included the people who were joining us.

CHAPTER 26

Ringing in the "Ewe" Year

As winter settled in, snow once again blanketed Homestead. Things slowed down, and I had learned to appreciate the peaceful quiet that January and February brought. I found I had more private time with all the animals, and the volunteers who helped during the winter were enjoying the quiet. Jordan continued to come out on Saturdays. I was amazed at how capable he was at tackling any project. He was able to move around Homestead at ease and had continued to build relationships with the animals. I had taught him how to care for the animals in a similar manner to the veterans' horse class; although he had access to all the animals. He excelled in school, and his relationship with his grandparents had improved greatly. He was taking on more responsibility with feeding and grooming, and the only chore he could not perform was mucking the stalls. It was because of this I did not hesitate when I got a call from Cody the last week of February.

It was midday, Saturday, February 24, and we had just finished lunch when the phone rang. It was Cody, and he was at one of the local sheep ranches. A first-time ewe was having difficulties in delivering, and the rancher had reached out to him for some help. Cody successfully delivered the triplets, but two of them appeared to have spider lamb syndrome (SLS), with their front legs being deformed. The rancher intended to destroy them, but Cody asked if he could make a call first. I hate when I am put in a position between taking an animal or their death, but coming from Cody, I knew it was true. I agreed to take the two lambs as long as he was willing to help me with their medical needs. The last lamb I had dealt with was when I was a kid, and it was an almost fully weaned big horn. I hung up the phone and turned to Jordan. When I told him we were expecting two newborn lambs, he jumped up and asked how he could help. While we waited on Cody to bring the lambs, Jordan called his grandparents and asked if he could stay and help tonight. I was a little surprised when they agreed. I wanted to make sure to thank them the next time I saw them. It was a big step in their relationship.

We decided to put them in the large barn and filled one of the stalls with straw. We added a couple of heat lamps to keep them warm and waited. When Cody arrived, we met him at his truck. He handed each of us a soft bundle and then went around to the back of his truck and grabbed some bottles and milk replacement. The rancher had agreed to supply us the bottles and milk after Cody told him about Homestead. We carried the lambs to the barn. They were so tiny; both had front legs that were twisted and bent at odd angles.

Cody told us that he had made sure they received their first meal from their mom in order to receive colostrum for their immune system, but because they had nursed, it might be harder to get them to take a bottle. He showed us how to mix the milk replacement and gently warm the nipple before trying to feed them. I handed Jordan a bottle and showed him how to hold the lamb for nursing. Fortunately, she took it immediately, and once again I saw the pure joy on Jordan's face. I grabbed the second bottle, and although she was a little more difficult, she settled down and took the bottle as well. As they nursed, I asked Cody about their legs. He told me many lambs that are born with SLS end up doing fine. If the structure supports their weight, they should able to walk; although it might be awkward. He said as they get older, depending on the severity of issues, there might be additional problems that we would need to monitor. It was hard for him to say right now, but he hoped they would get along just fine. All we could do was wait.

Cody thanked me again for taking them. He really was a very compassionate guy and cared about all animals. That was one of the reasons Dad had chosen him for the ranch vet when he opened his practice. Our previous vet was retiring, and he had told Dad about this new vet that was opening a large animal practice and a small animal clinic in the city. Dad set up a meeting with Cody and instantly liked the way he was around the horses. I am so glad he hired him. I know we would never have been successful at Homestead without his help.

We set up a feeding schedule for our newest additions, and I asked Jordan what he would like to name them. He told me he had no idea, so I asked him what they "looked" like to him. He thought for a moment and then said cotton candy.

I smiled and told him, "That was perfect. Meet Cotton and Candy."

We all laughed, and I asked Cody if he wanted to join us for dinner. I knew I had stuff to make homemade pizza, and when Cody agreed, I called Dad to invite him and Bill over for dinner so they could meet the lambs.

It was a nice evening just hanging out with everyone. Cody talked about his latest girlfriend, and Jordan asked questions about dating. We all spoke about some of our dating disasters, and after a lot of laughter, we checked on all the animals and finished the night with bottle feeding the lambs. After everyone left, Jordan asked to take the middle-of-the-night feeding, and I agreed to let him, knowing I would be up anyway to keep an eye on things. The next morning Jordan was up early. I asked him how the feeding had gone. He grinned and said I already knew. I guess I was not as sly as I had hoped. He said he was aware that I had watched over things. He had sensed me as much as heard me, but it was okay. He was only glad everything went well.

Jordan's grandparents arrived a little after morning chores to pick him up. Jordan took them out to the barn to meet Cotton and Candy. They were amused by the names, but I think they were more impressed by the way Jordan navigated Homestead. While Jordan took care of another bottle-feeding, I pulled his grandparents to the side. I thanked them for allowing Jordan to stay last night and help. When his grandpa spoke, it was to thank me. He said for the first time since their daughter's death, they felt like a family again. Jordan was a great kid, and what they all had been experiencing at Homestead was more than they could have hoped for. I told them I was glad they were part of our family now, and we would always look after each other. I then asked them about a surprise I had in store for Jordan if they would agree. It took little convincing, but they gave me their approval. I could not wait for a little-warmer weather.

CHAPTER 27

Saddle Up

By the middle of March, things had been warming up during the day. All the animals, including Cotton and Candy, were doing well. Both were standing and walking on their own. It reminded me of a giraffe's walk, but they did not seem to be in pain and were loving the attention from everyone. Eventually, we would move them to the other barn, but for now, they were small enough to stay where they were. Momma Moose and the twins were regularly spotted going in and out of the hut, but I knew soon enough they would move on. During one of my rides with Jolie, I saw Momma Moose appear at the edge of the woods. When she saw me, she took a few steps forward and looked toward me. I knew it was her way of saying goodbye, at least for now. I hoped to see her next winter.

I spoke to Dad after speaking to Jordan's grandparents, and I think he was as excited as I was about the surprise. On March 17 Homestead was decked out in green for St. Patrick's Day. Jordan was helping me finish up the morning chores, and I asked him if he wanted to go with me up to the stables. The temperature was supposed to get to fifty degrees, so I suggested we walk. I grabbed Jolie, and he went to track down Tapa.

As we headed to the stable, I asked him about plans for the summer. He told me if his grandparents agreed, he would like to spend more time at Homestead. I told him we could check with his grandparents, but I would like that too. When we arrived at the stable, Dad was already down at the arena. As we approached, Jordan said hi to Dad. He smiled and told Dad he recognized his aftershave. When there was a nicker from inside the arena, Jolie answered with one of her own. I asked Jordan if he remembered the first question he asked me. He shook his head, and I reminded him that he asked me if blind people rode.

I put my arm around his shoulder and led him into the arena, saying, "Jordan, meet Thunder."

It took a minute to sink in, and then Jordan began to shake. He wanted to know if he was really going to learn to ride. I told him yes, but we would take it slow. I explained that Thunder was a gelding, and he was one selected for the original veteran's group but had not been chosen. I described Thunder to him, telling him he was a bay, with a white star and two white socks. He stood almost sixteen hands high and was very gentle. He was experienced with riders, and we knew he would be a great horse for Jordan. We spent almost an hour going over the bridle, bit, and reins and how to put them on and take them off. I demonstrated how to do it and then had him do it.

When I was fairly sure he had it, we moved to the saddle and blanket. I described the black saddle with silver trim to him. While getting Thunder saddled, Dad had set up the mounting block. I explained to Jordan there were three steps. Dad would help him on the steps, and I would be holding Thunder. When Jordan was on top of the mounting block, I walked Thunder into place. We had Jordan reach out to feel Thunder and the saddle. We had him take hold of the saddle horn and then lift his right leg over the saddle. When he was sitting upright, we adjusted the stirrups and made sure he was comfortable with his positioning. I handed him the reins and explained to him how to maintain his balance. For the next hour, I led Thunder around the arena, allowing Jordan and Thunder a chance to get to know each other. The smile on Jordan's face said it all.

When we were finished, I led Thunder back to the mounting block, and Dad helped Jordan to dismount. I explained that after riding, especially for any length of time, Thunder needed to be cooled down and groomed. As we walked Thunder back to the stable, Jordan thanked me for the best day of his life. I smiled and told him we were just starting. If he was going to be hanging out at Homestead with me, he was going to need a horse and learn to ride. I told him Thunder was a gift from Dad and me if he was interested. He immediately wrapped his arms around me and said yes. Then he stopped and asked about his grandparents. When I told him that I had already spoken to them and they agreed, I was not sure who was more excited.

By the time we had finished with Thunder, Dad had called Jordan's grandparents and asked they pick him up at the stables. As they got out of their car, Jordan ran up to them, and they all embraced in a hug. I thought to myself, *This is what family means.* Jordan led them over to me and asked if it was okay for his grandparents to meet Thunder. I said absolutely as I accompanied them to his stall. Dad had taken a few pictures on his phone of Jordan riding, and he showed them to his grandparents. I could tell by their smiles how proud they were of him. I told Jordan we would continue the riding lessons on Saturday afternoons until he was out of school, then we could work on it during the week. I was anxious to get the two of them on the trails with Jolie and me. As much as I loved my quiet rides with Jolie, I was excited to have a riding buddy who could experience the trails in an entirely different way.

CHAPTER 28

Something in the Air

T
he remainder of spring and summer were filled with lots of laughter and love. Jordan was doing well with riding Thunder, and I loved the way he described his experience each time we returned. It was as if I was seeing the trails for the first time. He had been spending so much time at Homestead the extra bedroom had become his and now looked more like a teenage boy's room than a guest bedroom. I did not mind at all.

All the volunteers returned, along with a few new ones. David was working out great as part-time help at Bill's place, and he often accompanied Jordan and me on a ride using Kodiak. We started our second class for the veterans and ended up with twelve participants. The weekend crowds continued to grow, the highlights being the outrageous parties the volunteers continued to host.

The animals were amazing. Dakotah weighed in somewhere around one thousand three hundred pounds now, and Miracle had grown into a stunning filly. You would never know by her actions she was blind. Jolie and Kodiak kept an eye on her, but her confidence had grown by leaps and bounds. Pinky and Brain continued to entertain, and one of their favorite toys to pull around was an old rubber muck boot someone had left behind in their pasture. You could often see them playing tug of war. Liberty had reached just over three hundred fifty pounds, but Cody assured us she was healthy. With her refusal to eat pig feed and her diet of fresh fruits and vegetables, along with the human grains, he told us she would probably remain on the smaller side, which really was not disappointing to any of us. She had taken a liking to Cheez-It crackers, and you could always find a box or two nearby. BJ and Oscar loved the addition of Cotton and Candy to their pasture area.

To look out and see two goats, two lambs, and a pig, all playing together was a sight to behold. Tapa and Rebel continued to be inseparable most of the time. We had already ordered one new set of wheels for Rebel as he continued to grow. It would not be long before he required another. One of the boys from the accident had finally come out to see Rebel. He was around Jordan's age. He thanked me for everything I had done, and I could tell he really did care. He and Jordan had been spending some time together, and it was nice seeing their friendship develop.

Homestead, the ranch, and Bill's Boarding were doing well financially, but there were a few things that had continued to linger in the back of my mind. First, I noticed Joe had not been coming out as often. I reached out to Jerry and found out Joe's condition had officially been classified as Alzheimer's, and he had been moved into a memory-care unit. I was saddened by this turn of events and asked Jerry if it would be okay for me to go and see him and maybe bring him out to Homestead on occasion. He readily agreed and had me added to the list of visitors, as well as a person who could check Joe out on a day pass. I found myself going out to see Joe at least once a week. His decline was a bit startling. Many days he did not know who I was, so I would just sit and visit with him. I knew the mention of Kodiak's name would trigger some memory for him, and I would sit and listen to him revel in the stories over and over again. If he was having a good day, I would bring him out to Homestead for a visit and lunch. Admittedly, those were few and far between, but I loved to see his face light up when he saw Kodiak.

Another thing I noticed was Lisa and David seemed to be spending more and more time together. My feelings about this were hard to explain. I was happy for them. They really did deserve each other; yet there was something I could not put my finger on. It was one day when out riding Jolie, telling her about how I was feeling, that it

140

dawned on me. I was jealous. Not that I was interested in either one of them, but I was jealous that they had a relationship. I questioned why I was unable to find someone to love me. I always wanted to find a love like Mom and Dad, and now I was faced with that same type of love between David and Lisa. I knew I should not feel that way. I was surrounded by love. I had Dad and Bill. Jordan was as much a son to me as I could have ever wanted. The Homestead family emitted nothing but love to everyone. I was surrounded by love, and I was incredibly grateful, but I was still lonely.

July 4 fell on a Wednesday, so we decided to close Homestead on July 1 so we could have our annual Fourth of July barbecue for the volunteers. Everyone made it out sometime during the day. Jordan and his grandparents attended, as well as Cody and his "new" girlfriend. Danny stopped by for a beer, and David and Lisa made their relationship officially known. The business owners that had supported us throughout the year managed to stop by, and Sam told me Purina and his feedstore would continue to supply the grain. Jerry and his wife had brought Joe, along with one of his caregivers, Kasey. Joe was having a rough day, and I appreciated how Kasey took things in stride. I asked Joe if he wanted to see Kodiak, and I saw a moment of recognition. Joe had been using a wheelchair by now, so Kasey pushed him toward the barn. Kodiak immediately acknowledged him with a welcoming nicker. Kasey rolled Joe in front of the stall so Kodiak could drop his head down for Joe to pet. We stepped back and allowed the two of them a few minutes alone. Kasey told me how impressive Homestead was and asked for a tour at some point in the future. I readily agreed and provided my phone number, saying, "Call whenever." I just hoped it would not be too long of a wait.

PART 6

Losing Balance

CHAPTER 29

Saying Goodbye

On August 15 I received a call from Jerry. Joe had passed away in his sleep. Although I was not surprised, it was still a shock. No matter what you do, you are never prepared for death. Jerry told me they were planning the funeral services for the weekend, and he was wondering if maybe they could do a memorial service at Homestead. He told me that Joe had often referred to Homestead as not only a sanctuary for Kodiak but for himself. I told him how sorry I was for his loss, and of course, we would be honored to have a memorial service for Joe. We talked for a few more minutes, both of us fighting back the tears, and decided Sunday afternoon would give us enough time to get things in order.

When I hung up, I could not fight the tears any longer. When Jordan entered the cabin, he knew something was wrong. I told him about Joe, and we sat together for a few minutes, sharing our memories. Afterward I called Lisa and asked for her help in getting things organized. I knew I could count on her. I called Dad next and then a few of the other volunteers who had been close to Joe. A little later in the evening, I received a call from Kasey, just checking in and to make sure I knew about Joe. I said yes and then told Kasey about the memorial service. After what I saw in July, I knew Joe would want Kasey to be there.

Jerry had arranged a small funeral, which I attended, and afterward we headed for Homestead. Although the funeral was private, everyone had been invited to the memorial service. Brad and Carla had helped Jerry with the obituary and made sure it was prominent in the newspaper. The memorial service was surprisingly uplifting and well-attended. Lisa had arranged for a caterer to provide the food. Everyone had pulled photos together that had been taken of Joe, and several photo boards and framed photos were set on tables.

After the minister spoke, Jerry got up and reminded everyone that it was a celebration of Joe's life. He asked that we share memories of his dad and that death was not the end. I had a few words prepared, but when I got up there, I wadded the notes up and spoke from my heart. I told everyone about the first time I met Joe and how both he and Kodiak had joined the Homestead family. I spoke about taking Joe out riding on Kodiak for what I now knew was his last ride, and I spoke about what Joe had meant to me. When I managed to choke out the last words, I looked up to see Kasey in the back. Our eyes met for only a moment, but I knew then I was looking into the eyes of my future.

As I looked around, there did not appear to be a dry eye. When I stepped down, a few others offered some kind words and some funny stories; but honestly, I do not remember what was said. I made my way to the back and took hold of Kasey's hand. When everyone was finished speaking, we sat down to eat. The minister blessed the meal, and what followed was a true celebration. As people started to leave, Jerry approached me and asked if he could speak to me. We stepped off to the side, and he asked what would happen to Kodiak now. I told him Kodiak would always be a part of Homestead. He then told me that one of Joe's wishes had been for someone to love Kodiak as much as he had. Joe had told Jerry several months earlier that he had seen that love between David and Kodiak. I knew what Jerry was asking, and I understood the bond between David and Kodiak. I asked Jerry if he wanted to go with me and talk to David.

We pulled David aside and told him of Joe's wish. I could see in David's eyes both his sorrow and his gratitude. We stood talking for a few more minutes before Jerry needed to get back to say more goodbyes. As David and I walked back, he put his arm on my shoulder and thanked me. I just nodded, but he proceeded to tell me he was not just thanking me for Kodiak. He was thanking me for creating a place where he felt at home. I thought about it and realized Homestead had become a home for so many. David wandered off to go find Lisa and tell her the news. I looked around, but Jordan told me Kasey had to leave to go to work. I managed to get through the rest of the evening with Tapa by my side. When I finally made it back to the cabin, I looked at my phone. I had missed a text message from earlier. It was from Kasey, apologizing for having to leave. It was followed by two words and an emoji. The two words were, "I know," and the emoji was fireworks. It brought a smile to my face, and I returned the text with an apology, stating I just saw my phone. I followed up, saying next time a proper tour of Homestead was in order.

CHAPTER 30

Kasey

ide note: I wrote, deleted, and rewrote this chapter, not sure if I would include it in the final draft. In the end, I figured I had already shared so much about myself; I might as well share this too. For anyone who knows the true meaning of love at first sight, you will understand what a blubbering idiot it turns us into.

It was a week after the memorial service before Kasey could make it back out to Homestead. I felt the excitement of a little kid on Christmas morning. I had not shared my feelings with anyone but Jolie, but I think Jordan had some idea. Not that cleaning the cabin, making sure it was stocked with healthy food, and ironing my clothes were any type of hint. It was not like I never dated, and I certainly was not a virgin, but this was different. I was nervous.

Kasey pulled up in a black Chevy Avalanche. It fit. The sleek black design matched Kasey's dark hair and eyes. I approached with a wave, saying, "Hi." Kasey responded with, "Hi." Then there was this awkward silence, the kind when you are not sure what to say. We had been talking on the phone every night, and now it seemed like we had no idea what to say to each other.

I finally broke the silence, saying, "Let me show you around."

Tapa had followed me outside and was already standing next to me. I reached down and introduced him to Kasey. When we entered the main barn, Kasey walked over and patted Dakotah on the head. I started to relax a little and began sharing the stories of all the animals.

Kasey asked if it would be all right to enter the stall with Miracle. I said, "Of course," and opened it. Kasey reached out, and Miracle sniffed the hand before nuzzling. I handed Kasey a couple of peppermints that Miracle quickly accepted. I went over to Jolie and placed my arm on her neck, giving her a couple of peppermints as well. I told Kasey her rescue story. I was not ready for the other discussion yet. Kasey met and provided treats to Kodiak, Pinky, and Brain before we headed out to the small barn. Kasey asked how big of a place I had, so I explained, all together there were nine hundred acres that were owned by Dad, Bill, and me. On the property were Homestead, the ranch, and Bill's place. I explained we had a lot of acreage that we planted in alfalfa, and the remaining acreage was wooded.

Just before we got to the barn, we were met with a very rowdy BJ. When I saw him and realized he was outside the pen, I shouted, "BJ!" at which time he proceeded to faint. At first Kasey looked on in horror but then realized what had happened. As we both laughed, we went to get BJ and placed him back in the pen. I introduced Oscar, Liberty, Cotton, and Candy. After playing with "the littles," as some of the volunteers had started calling them, we headed back to the cabin.

I said, "How about a beer?" and went inside to grab a couple and let Rebel out.

He immediately bounded for Kasey, who reached down and picked him up. We sat on the front porch, and Kasey asked about my son. I was confused at first. When I realized we were talking about Jordan, I explained that Jordan was not my biological son and shared his story. I said that although Jordan might not be my actual son, I often thought of him that way. When asked where he was, I said he was at his grandparents.

We spent the rest of the evening talking about other things like parents and where Kasey grew up, which happened to be in Oregon. When I asked how someone from Oregon ended up in Montana, the answer was family. Kasey's grandfather, Max, lived in Montana; and when he was unable to care for himself or his farm, Kasey came out to lend a hand. Max had ended up in the same assisted-living facility as Joe. Kasey signed up as a caregiver for Max, but when he died, one of the patients Kasey had been assigned was Joe. Joe was a lot like her grandfather, so Kasey stayed for a while. Kasey planned on heading back to Oregon after Joe's death. That was until Joe's memorial service.

Kasey then asked how I ended up at Homestead. I went to grab another beer; this was going to be a long story, and I knew at some point, I would have to bring up my leg. Most of the time I never thought about it anymore. But now, with Kasey sitting on the front porch, I did not know what I was going to say. As I started to walk out with the beers, Kasey tapped on the door, needing to use the bathroom. After looking at me, Kasey said maybe it would be better to leave. I reached out and said no, but there were a few things I needed to share.

After Kasey returned to the porch, I proceeded to talk about the Army. I was just finishing my beer when I finished my story and reached down to pull up the leg of my jeans. I looked down, not sure what to say. Kasey reached over and took my hand. As I looked into Kasey's eyes, I was not exactly sure what I saw. Was it pity, concern, fear, apprehension, or some other horrible feeling? I stood to turn away, but Kasey stopped me. The next thing I knew, we were in each other's arms, kissing. I am not sure how long we were there on the porch, but when Kasey pulled away, I knew I was not the only one who felt something. Kasey said it was time to head home.

As much as I would have liked to spend the night together, I knew we needed time to process what was happening. Another kiss, and Kasey headed down the drive. I went back inside the cabin, and a few minutes later, a fireworks emoji appeared on my phone. I returned it with an emoji of my own. For the next couple of months, Kasey and I saw each other when we could. We both were busy, finding time to talk every night, but we had not really been alone since that evening in August.

On October 6 Kalispell had a rodeo coming to town. We all planned to go. Jordan "decided" he would ride with Dad and Bill. He and Kasey got along great, and I think he knew we needed some time alone. Kasey met me at Homestead after work, just as I was finishing the afternoon chores. We decided to take the Jeep as it was still warm, and the doors were off. Kasey had packed a cooler and loaded it in the Jeep. I said I needed to grab a quick shower, and I would be out in ten minutes. I had laid out new jeans and polished my black cowboy boots. I was standing in the shower, letting the warm water wash away all the grime, when I heard the door open. As I looked out, there stood Kasey naked. I had no time to think before the two of us were in the shower together. All I will say is, we never made it to the rodeo, and it seemed no one was surprised.

CHAPTER 31

The Past

It was nearing Halloween when an older car came down the drive early in the morning. The sun was barely up, and I was there alone. I reached for my gun, more out of habit than anything else. As I stepped out of the cabin door, the car came to a stop, and a very distinguished man, maybe sixty to sixty-five, stepped out from the car. He asked if I was the owner of Homestead Sanctuary. I told him "technically" I was the owner and that we would be open to the public on the weekend. He told me his name was Jackson, and he was hoping he could speak to me for a few minutes. He reminded me of a businessman, but I agreed to speak to him. I offered him a chair on the porch, and we sat down. He asked if there was a horse at the sanctuary by the name of Ma Jolie. I am sure I looked stunned for a minute; no one used her full name around here. I finally told him yes, she was here. The minute I said she was here, he transformed from a stoic businessman to a man who looked like he was about to cry. He told me that yesterday he had arrived in town and had gone out to the ranch where she had been kept. He was told about the fire and that they were not sure if the horse had lived or not. For the next couple of hours, he told me the story of Ma Jolie.

He and his wife, Nicole, used to live up near Eureka. They had a small spread up there with about sixty acres. He was a lawyer, and his wife a schoolteacher. They both loved horses, and for their twenty-fifth anniversary, he had given his wife Ma Jolie. They had been having a magical life until about ten years ago when Nicole was diagnosed with multiple sclerosis (MS). For several years she was treated locally, but unfortunately, her condition continued to deteriorate. Her one joy in life was riding Ma Jolie. As her ability to ride declined, a friend began coming out and working with Ma Jolie, training her on lowering herself to the ground and then getting up with a rider. With the training, Nicole was able to ride even after she became confined to a wheelchair. In late 2013 Nicole qualified for a clinically trial at Memorial Healthcare Institute for Neuroscience in Owosso, Michigan. It had been a difficult decision, but they really had no choice. They sold their place and moved to Michigan in order to participate in the trial. They had placed Ma Jolie and Jackson's horse with a friend who had apparently sold them to the stable in Whitefish. He had spent the past week trying to track down the location in Whitefish, only to be disappointed yesterday.

When he reached this point in his story, I asked if he would like to see Jolie. He told me yes, but he needed to tell me the rest of the story first. He said his wife was under hospice care now, and her only wish had been to reconnect with Ma Jolie. He knew we would be unable to travel to Michigan, but he was hoping we could use FaceTime or another video connection so his wife could see Ma Jolie.

I knew that we had to find a way to make this happen, so I reached out to Lisa. I told her a condensed version of the story, and she said she would be out within the hour. I told Jackson that Lisa was an IT expert, and she would arrive shortly. After that, we headed to the barn so he could see Jolie for himself. As we entered the barn, she let out her familiar nicker. As Jackson approached her, I knew she recognized him. Once he saw her, the tears began to fall. A few minutes later, we stepped out of the barn, and he made a phone call. I did not want to intrude, but I could tell he must have been talking to a caregiver, and then eventually, he must have spoken to his wife. I heard him tell her that he had found Ma Jolie and to hang on, we were going to find a way for her to see her.

Lisa arrived shortly after with some video equipment and an iPad. I introduced her to Jackson, and she asked what type of device his wife was using. He told her she had access to an iPhone and an iPad. Lisa wanted to set up outside where the lighting was better. We could do a video connection, and she could also do a full video that Jackson could take with him. While she set up, I saddled Jolie. Lisa got the phone number to the iPad from Jackson once she was set up.

When the video call connected, I walked up with Jolie. I could see Nicole propped up in a hospital bed. It was obvious she was in pain. I could not see very well, but I turned Jolie to face Nicole. Jolie let out a nicker, and I saw a smile on Nicole's face. I heard Nicole say something, but I could not make out what she had said. Jackson asked her to repeat it, and he managed to figure out she said ride. Jackson told me she wanted to see Jolie move. I removed my prosthetic, and Jolie dropped to the ground. I could tell Jackson was surprised, but I did not want to take time to explain. Lisa ensured Nicole could see Jolie and kept the video on her. We went through a walk, trot, canter, and then a run. I came back up to the iPad, and I could see the joy in her eyes. I looked at Jackson and asked if he wanted to ride. He nodded, so I dismounted; and when Jolie stood up, I gave Jackson a leg up. I adjusted his stirrups and let him enjoy a ride. I got to watch Nicole's face as Jackson rode. I could only imagine what she was thinking. When Jackson circled back around, he came up and dismounted. He walked Jolie over to the iPad, and they said goodbye. He told her that he would be home soon.

Lisa got Jackson's e-mail and told him he would have the full video by the end of the day. She packed everything up and headed back to work. Jackson walked with me as we took Jolie back to her stall and cooled her down. I asked when he was leaving, and he said he had a flight out later that night. He thanked me for everything, and I told him if he was ever back this way to please stop in and say hi. He told me he was glad Jolie had a wonderful home, and he could tell how much I cared. He told me he knew Nicole was thrilled to see how well Jolie looked, and whatever time she had left, they would have the video to enjoy together. I never heard from Jackson after that day, not that I expected to, but I always hoped that something changed, and one day he and Nicole would stop by.

CHAPTER 32

The Accident

The weather had been unusually cooperative this past summer, and it looked like we were going to get a fourth cut on the alfalfa. We knew we needed to restack what we had in the hay loft to make room. I told Dad I would be up after morning chores, and we could unload some of the hay from the hay loft and move it over to Homestead. Bill was going to take a load out to his place for the winter as well.

When I arrived at the farmhouse, Dad's truck was in the drive, but I did not see him. I thought maybe he had already headed to the stable and was waiting on me. When I arrived, I still did not see him, so I tried to call, but it went to voice mail. I could tell Dad had been there, and he had already started throwing hay down, even though I had told him to wait. As I started to walk out, I heard something. I was not sure what it was, but it was coming from the hay on the ground. As I got closer, I realized it was Dad. He had apparently fallen when he was tossing the hay and was somewhat buried underneath. I grabbed my phone and dialed 911 and gave them the address. I got to Dad and cleared some of the hay from on top of him, but I was afraid to move him. He was conscious, but I could tell he was in a lot of pain. I sat with him and called Bill. When he answered, I told him what happened. He said he would be right there, but I suggested he meet us at the hospital instead; I could hear the ambulance as it approached.

When the EMTs arrived, they checked vitals and checked for trauma. They told me Dad had been fortunate, since there had been some hay to break his fall. He did not appear to have a head injury, but they were concerned with a possible back injury, so they placed him on a backboard before transporting him to the hospital. I called Kasey and then followed behind the ambulance.

Arrival at any hospital is chaotic, but when you have a stubborn, old man who insisted he was all right, it made it worse. The doctors finally convinced him that he needed X-rays. Bill arrived just as they were taking him for the X-rays, and he asked what had happened. I told him, from what I could tell, Dad had started tossing the hay down before I arrived. He must have slipped when tossing a bale down and ended up falling. I had no idea how long he had been lying on the stable floor. Bill said that sounded about right. Dad had mentioned to him that he really did not want me up in the loft with my leg, so he probably thought he would get it down before I got there. I knew Bill did not mean anything by what he said, but I immediately felt the guilt. It was like a stake through the heart, thinking Dad was in the hospital because of me. As we sat there, I started questioning everything I was doing. Maybe I could not do the work for the ranch or Homestead. Maybe I was just trying to overcompensate, and I was putting others, like Dad, at risk. What would I do if something happened to Dad? Kasey arrived before Dad was back from X-ray. It was obvious something was going on, and Kasey quickly pulled me into a hug. In a calm and quiet voice, I heard, "I got you." I let myself relax into the embrace.

Dad returned to the emergency room, and shortly after the doctor arrived. The news was not good. Dad had broken his hip and was going to require surgery. They were working on getting him scheduled, but in the meantime, he would be moved onto the orthopedic floor. They had given Dad something for pain, and he was in and out of sleep.

After we had Dad settled into a room, the doctor came back and told us his surgery would be scheduled for the next afternoon. He told us to expect Dad to be in the hospital for four to five days. When he was released to go home, someone would need to be with him for the following four to six weeks. Someone would need to help him get around and to take him to his physical therapy appointments. Kasey immediately jumped in and offered to help. So did Bill. I would need to figure out a schedule to care for Dad as well as take care of the ranch and Homestead.

I stayed with Dad until visiting hours were over. Kasey had gone back to work from the hospital but would be at Homestead later that night. I had sent Bill home, but he said he would be available for whatever I needed him to do. On the drive home, I tried to work out the details. I knew the first thing we needed to do would be move the hay from the loft. I called David and found that Bill had already filled him in. I asked him if he would be able to meet me early in the morning at the stable so we could start moving the hay. I could only work a few hours since I needed to be back at the hospital before Dad's surgery, but I thought I might be able to make some progress. He agreed, so we planned on meeting at 6:00 a.m.

When I got home, Kasey was already there and so was Jordan. Kasey had called him and asked if he would be able to come out after school to help with the animals. When Kasey explained what had happened, Jordan spoke to his grandparents, and they agreed to bring him over. When I walked in, there was pizza and a beer waiting. As I ate, Jordan told me he had spoken to his grandparents, and he would be missing school the next day. He wanted to be at the hospital with me for Dad's surgery. Kasey had also taken off work. We decided that Kasey and Jordan could take care of Homestead in the morning, and I would go to the ranch. Hopefully, David and I could get the old hay distributed to Homestead and Bill's barn. I would then come home and clean up, and we would take the Avalanche and the Jeep to the hospital. By taking both trucks, I could stay at the hospital, and Jordan and Kasey would be able to come back and take care of Homestead that evening. That was as much as my brain could handle for the day. I finished dinner and then headed for a shower and bed. Kasey and Jordan locked everything up, and everyone called it a night.

As we laid in bed, Kasey asked what was going on at the hospital, knowing it was more than Dad's injury. I explained the comment

Bill had made and how I was questioning if I should be doing all this. Kasey rolled over and laid an arm across my chest, "Do not let others determine your limitations." Kasey was right; it was exactly what I needed to hear.

The next morning we were all up early. I decided to ride Jolie up to the ranch. I could hook the trailer up to Dad's truck to move the hay, and I really needed the quiet time with Jolie to process everything that had happened in the past twenty-four hours. I arrived at the ranch about 5:45 a.m. and put Jolie in a stall. I grabbed Dad's keys and took the truck over to hook up the trailer. Just as I was finishing, I saw David pulling in, followed by several more cars and trucks. I was a little confused until I saw the people getting out of the vehicles. Apparently, David had called all the veterans that had been part of our horse program and asked for help. All in, there were about twenty people. With that many hands, it did not take us long to get hay to both Bill's barn and to Homestead. When we loaded up the last of it, I thanked everyone for coming out and helping. When someone asked about the next cut, I told them the cutting and baling would not be an issue. We had machinery for that, but I might need some help filling and stacking the hay loft. I agreed, after some coercion, that I would let them know when we were ready.

We arrived at the hospital shortly before Dad went back for pre-op. Bill had been there most of the morning. Dad was in and out of consciousness. I was certain he was on some strong painkillers. I explained to Bill what we had accomplished that morning. He was impressed, but not surprised, that the veterans had shown up. I told him they agreed to come back when we were ready to load the hay loft up with the new hay. About that time, they came to take Dad back to surgery, so we all moved into the waiting room. The surgery lasted a little longer than expected, but when the doctor came out to speak to us, he said it went very well. Bill stayed until Dad was back in his room. Kasey and Jordan stayed until he was a little more alert. Jordan really wanted to stay longer, but I told him I trusted him to show Kasey what needed to be done at Homestead before Kasey took him home. He reluctantly agreed, and I told him he could spend more time with Dad on the weekend and once he got home.

The next few days were about the same. Dad was feeling better and was pushing the doctors to let him go home. Before they would release him, they needed to know who would be staying with him. When I sat down with Bill and Kasey, we decided the easiest way would be for Bill to spend the overnight shift with Dad. David had agreed to stay at Bill's and would take care of things there as well as help at the ranch. Since Kasey worked a variety of shifts, we would split the days and evenings. Jordan was going to come by every day after school to spend time with Dad and would also accompany me on whatever weekend shift I would be covering. Either Kasey or I would take care of cooking and having meals ready. We set up his reoccurring physical therapy for 10:00 a.m. so we could finish any morning chores before we had to leave. I knew it wouldn't leave a lot of daylight hours for Kasey and I to see each other, but we would make it work. When we told Dad how we were going to work it out, he was not happy. Not happy might be an understatement. His exact words were, "I don't need no damn babysitter!" The doctor told him if he would not agree to what we had planned, he would send him to a rehabilitation home. With that threat, Dad agreed to let someone stay with him.

For the first couple of weeks, things were going fine. By week three, Dad was being less gracious. I knew he was used to being active, and sitting around the farmhouse was killing him. More than once we had caught him trying to make his way to the stables. The third week I had managed to get all the alfalfa cut and was working on baling. Bill was spending most of his time with Dad, and David was helping whenever he could. We made plans to move the hay into the hay loft on Saturday, and I sent a message out to the veterans, asking for help.

By now, we were a week away from Thanksgiving, and I had not even given it a thought. When Lisa asked if I thought Dad might be up for some visitors, I assured her he was probably more than ready to see some faces besides ours. She suggested that we do our annual Thanksgiving open house at the farmhouse but that she and the vol-unteers would do all the planning, cooking, and cleanup. At first, I declined; but the more I thought about it, I decided it might be just what Dad needed.

Thanksgiving was a wonderful success, and I was right; it was just what Dad needed. As much as he said he hated all the attention, I knew deep down he loved it. The older volunteer women were doting on him, and he was eating it up. The food was amazing, and best of all, I hadn't had to cook. Kasey and I finally were able to spend an entire day together, and I knew I had a lot to be thankful for this year. The last few months had been very tough and had thrown me off-balance more than once. But I also realized, through it all, I had been able to regain my balance at Homestead. With Jolie, Tapa, and now Kasey and Jordan by my side, I knew I could deal with whatever life threw my way.

PART 7

Balancing on the Circle

CHAPTER 33

The Calm

Christmas was an incredibly quiet time this year. With Dad still recuperating from his surgery, we decided a traditional Christmas was in order. Of course, we still decorated Homestead, and the community Christmas tree was bigger and better than the year before. Jordan and his grandparents had added their own special ornaments, and Kasey had a special one created for the two of us. We continued the tradition of handmade ornaments for the volunteers, but we held off on having a party. It had been a long year, and it seemed to be time to sit back and just enjoy the quiet.

We planned a nice Christmas Day with Jordan and his grandparents, David and Lisa, Dad, Bill, and of course, Kasey and me. We agreed on a small gift exchange, nothing elaborate. After finishing up the morning chores at Homestead, we packed a few things up and headed for the farmhouse. Everyone planned to be there around 2:00 p.m., and dinner would be at 4:00 p.m. As I stood on the front porch, I heard the familiar call of Momma Moose. She was back again this year, but the twins must have moved on. I had seen her on a couple of occasions and had been putting grain out for the past month.

I walked over to the main barn and stood in the doorway. I looked around at all the amazing animals that now called Homestead their home. I smiled as I thought about all their stories. I walked to the small barn and took in all the "littles" even if they were not so little anymore. The love they received from everyone could not compare to the love they had given. The word that came to mind was "unconditional." People seem to place conditions on their love, but animals never do. I walked back over to the cabin and saw Kelsey getting Rebel's Christmas sweater on him. I had no idea how I had gotten so lucky. Tapa bounded toward me, tongue hanging out, decked out in his own sweater. I reached down and patted the almost-white fur.

Encircling Kasey's waist with my arms, I whispered, "Unconditionally."

We loaded the boys into the Jeep, along with Rebel's wheels, Christmas gifts, and food, and made our way to the farmhouse. Bill was already there; I had noticed he had been spending a lot more time with Dad at the farmhouse. By the time we unloaded, David and Lisa arrived. We helped them unload and walked inside. Dad had already started a fire in the fireplace, and I believe he and Bill had already been into the eggnog. Within the next half hour, Jordan and his grandparents arrived. Before we even made it to the door to help them, Jordan burst through the door, shouting, "Merry Christmas!" He was decked out in a full Santa Clause suit, complete with white beard and hat. As we went to help bring things in from their car, we all agreed it was a very Merry Christmas.

As I sat at the dinner table, I looked at all the faces of the people I had grown to love and thought back to the movie, *It's a Wonderful Life,* and realized how close several of us had been to dying and how the reason for others being here was due to someone they loved dying. I was lost in thought when Kelsey reached for my hand and brought me back to the present.

After dinner, everyone pitched in, and we did dishes and cleaned up the kitchen. We were all so full, except for Jordan, we waited to have dessert. Jordan had commented on the chocolate pie that Dad had made from the time he arrived. He told Dad that he could just smell how "dope" it was going to be. When he said it, I had to explain to Dad, Bill, and his grandparents that it really was okay and just meant it was going to be good. I may not have known much teen slang, but at least I got that one right. When we were finished cleaning up, Dad told Jordan to go ahead and cut himself a piece, and with that, a quarter of the pie was gone. His grandmother started to say something, but I reached over and shook my head. I told her there was another one in the refrigerator, and we should let him enjoy this Christmas.

After dinner, we moved into the living room and decided it was time to open some presents. Everyone seemed to be keeping with the theme of reasonable items. Socks, clothing, books, and music were common themes. I had given Jordan a subscription to Audible and had purchased a few of my favorite books for him. I was looking forward to sharing thoughts when he had finished listening to them.

As we were nearing the end of the presents, I saw Dad look to Bill and nod his head. Bill spoke up and said he had an announcement to make. He had all our attention now. He proceeded to tell us that he and Dad had been talking and that he was going to be moving into the farmhouse with Dad. He explained that since the accident, he had been spending a lot of time with Dad. It reminded both when they were little and how much fun they had growing up. He then looked at David and told him, if he was interested, he would like him to consider moving into his house on a permanent basis. He would be willing to work out the details on how David could buy the house and, if he wanted, buy into ranch operations. He and Dad then offered David a full-time job. They told David they did not need an answer right then, and he could let them know.

To be honest, I was a little upset that Bill and Dad had not discussed this with me. I really liked David; he was family. But I also had been handling the business, and as a stakeholder, I felt I should have been in the loop. Kasey reached over and took my hand, knowing I was upset. I let the calm pass over me. I would talk to them later.

I could see the excitement in David's eyes. He said he would let them know soon. He reached over and picked up a small package and handed it to Lisa. As she opened the package, I could see it was a small jewelry box. As she opened it, I saw the look of surprise on her face. David bent down onto one knee and took the box from her hands. He removed the ring and made one of the sweetest proposals I have heard. He told her that he had been searching his whole life for someone like her, and although he didn't have all the answers, he knew he would find them with her by his side. When she said yes, we all applauded. Then he turned to Dad and Bill and told them he would love to discuss the possibility of buying Bill's house and investing in the ranch.

Throughout all this activity, Kasey held firm to my hand. The effect kept me grounded, and I finally realized that I was happy for David and Lisa, and the other stuff really did not matter. Having David around full-time would certainly help with the ranch work, and Lisa being around all the time would make it easier on Homestead too. We celebrated with a toast. By the end of the night, it was decided Bill would move into the farmhouse when the weather warmed up a little. His horse would move into the stable. When David, along with Lisa, moved into Bill's house, we would move Kodiak out there. We could then move Thunder from the stable over to Homestead. As the night ended, everyone agreed it had been a special Christmas we would all remember for a long time.

CHAPTER 34

Year of the Pig

I do not know when the "mini" or "teacup" craze started, but apparently, if was in full swing by spring. It was the year of the pig according to the Chinese New Year, and apparently, Montana was taking it seriously. I have no idea what people were thinking, and their total lack of research on raising a pig befuddles me to this day. We had very peaceful start to the year when the phone calls started. The first call was from a woman who told me she had purchased a teacup pig, and now it weighed sixty pounds, and there was no way she could keep it. I knew nothing about pigs other than what I had learned from Liberty.

I did some quick research and found many unethical breeders were selling piglets to people, promising they would remain tiny. It took very little research for me to find that on average, these pigs grow to be sixty to one hundred fifty pounds. Apparently, this was a problem across the country and had recently shown up in Montana. Within a couple of weeks, I had received dozens of calls. These pigs must have been common Christmas gifts the previous year, and now they were reaching full size. Many people were wanting to get rid of them. I had been able to locate a couple of rescue groups and started referring callers to them.

One evening, when Kasey stopped by after work, I saw what looked to be a pet carrier in the back of the truck. When I walked out, Kasey opened the tailgate and brought the carrier to the ground.

When I approached, I realized I was looking at one of these so-called mini pigs. Kasey explained that the carrier had been sitting at the end of the drive near the Homestead sign. It obviously had been dumped. Thank goodness Kasey came by because the pig probably would not have survived the night. I called the police to make a report and called Cody. He agreed to stop by the next day, and for tonight, he advised to feed the pig the same dinner we would give Liberty. He would bring out a bag of mini-pig feed tomorrow. We brought the carrier inside, and both Tapa and Rebel immediately showed an interest. I had to admit, I was curious too. We went into the kitchen and closed the door. Kasey reached down and opened the carrier, and out popped this not-so-little black-and-white pig. It was cute, with a short snout and a rounded belly. It walked up to Kasey and let out a little snort. Kasey dropped to the floor, and the thirty-plus-pound pig crawled into the inviting lap. I think I knew then; I was in trouble.

I sat in the kitchen, looking up more information on mini pigs, and it seemed this one was a Vietnamese Pot-bellied Pig. I found that many people had pot-bellied pigs, and they could be trained to use a litter box. It was too cold for it to be outside if it had been living inside, so I was hoping that whoever dumped it had kept it indoors as I set up a litter box. We were in luck. It immediately used the litter box and let out another squeal. Not knowing how long it had been sitting at the end of the drive, I grabbed some fruits, veggies, and a few Cheerios, mixing up a little dinner for our new guest. For tonight, it would stay in the kitchen.

Cody stopped by the next morning. He confirmed she was a potbelly and estimated her to be a little over a year old. He went ahead and vaccinated her since we had no history on her, and he asked what I was going to do with her. I told him I did not know yet. He told me it would be okay to introduce her to Tapa and Rebel but to watch for any signs of aggression. Cody agreed to help me, and we decided the barn was the best neutral space for the introduction. I still had Liberty's original harness, so I placed it on the pig, and we went out to the barn.

All the animals greeted us as we entered. Jolie let out a nicker, and the pig returned with a grunt. It almost sounded as if they had their own language. Cody stayed with the pig while I went to get the boys. Rebel was on his third set of wheels now and had grown to almost sixty pounds while Tapa had leveled off at seventy. I entered the barn, as if we were on our morning visit, hoping for the best. For the first few minutes, things stayed calm, the dogs approaching and sniffing the pig. Cody reached down and took the leash off the pig, and the next minute we had a pig in a full-out piggy run, chasing the pups around the barn. There was barking, there was grunting, and there was complete chaos for several minutes. I was trying to grab the pups while Cody reached for the pig. While all this was going on, Kasey had snuck in unnoticed. With a loud, "Hey!" from Kasey, everything just stopped. The pig looked up and immediately went over to Kasey and plopped over for a belly rub. Cody and I just looked at each other. The pups came up to me, looking as confused as I was feeling. Cody handed Kasey the leash for the pig and walked out of the barn, laughing. In that moment, I think everyone knew the real boss.

When we all were back in the cabin, I asked Kasey what we should do with the pig. I had spoken to one of the rescues who would be willing to take her, but I needed to know if Kasey was willing to give her up. By the end of the evening, we had decided "Arryn" would be staying, but we would be building a separate area outdoors for her kingdom. For now, she would stay in the cabin but would only be around the boys when supervised.

Less than a week later, I got a call from Danny. He was on his way to a small farm. The report said there were multiple animals, and it was reported as abuse. He asked if I could meet him there, not knowing what he was going to find. He had already called Nate from the dog/cat shelter, and he was on his way too.

When I arrived, Danny and the police were already there. Nate arrived a few minutes later. When we looked around, it was obvious the property had been set up for dog-fighting. Initially, we found eight dogs in various conditions and multiple pens. Several were going to require immediate medical care. As we continued to the furthest part of the property, we came upon another small enclosure. As we got closer, I heard the familiar sound of grunting pigs. There was no way I could have imagined what I saw when we opened the enclosure. The only way I could describe it would be coming across a Humvee that had been blown apart. The stench, along with all the blood, nearly made me vomit. There was no doubt he was using the pigs to train the dogs. When we finally got to the back of the enclosure, we found two small pigs covered in feces and blood with what looked like infected bite wounds. They were terrified and huddled in the corner. I walked out of the enclosure and called Cody.

When he answered, I found out Nate had already called him, and he was on his way. I told him about the pigs and asked if he had a crate with him. He assured me he had enough and would be there within thirty minutes. While I waited, all I could think of was, what kind of monster could do this to animals? Danny told me the police were filing charges, and he let me know I might be called to testify. He asked if I could make sure Cody did a full report on the pigs' and dogs' conditions, and everyone needed to take lots of photos. When Cody arrived, Danny told him the same thing and then asked him to forward all reports.

It took several hours to get all the animals loaded up. Nate took all the dogs back to the rescue, and I took the pigs directly to Cody's clinic. He was going to take care of the pigs first and then grab everything he needed to take over to Nate's. When we carried the pigs in, the first thing he wanted to do was get them cleaned up. Donning heavy gloves, we reached into the crate and grabbed the pigs. Placing them into bathing tubs, we began bathing them. Surprisingly, they were very docile, probably in shock. I noticed as we started washing away the dirt and blood that they did not look like Arryn. Their snouts were longer and were missing the big, round belly. They were longer and reminded me of a small Liberty.

Once they were clean, I noticed their coloring was different as well. They had more spots, like a paint horse. When I asked Cody, he told me they looked like Juliana pigs but admitted he was no pig expert. While he was treating all their wounds, he told me that he had heard some of the dog-fighting rings had been taking in the small pigs that people were getting rid of and then using them as bait for the fighting dogs. I was appalled by what he was telling me. These poor pigs were bought as pets, and when they got bigger than what the owners were promised, they found themselves being mauled by vicious dogs.

When Cody finished, he told me these pigs were male, and both were somewhere around two years old. After looking up images of Juliana pigs on my phone, I decided Cody was right. They both were just under fifty pounds, and I found that Juliana pigs were known as "spotted" pigs, explaining their markings. Cody sent me home with antibiotics and instructions to try to keep them both quiet. The injuries were treatable, but he had a big concern around the infection. I loaded up the pigs and helped Cody load up supplies to take to Nate's rescue. In my head, I was trying to figure out where to go with the two newest residents when my phone rang. It was Kasey, asking me if I was on my way. I then looked at my watched and realized what time it was. I apologized as date night needed to be canceled. I explained the situation about the pigs. Kasey agreed to pick up Chinese food and meet me at Homestead.

Kasey reached the cabin before I did and had already gone into the main barn. Jordan was there as well, and the two of them had cleared out a stall and laid down fresh straw. They had prepared a couple of food bowls and fresh water. I brought the pigs into the barn and released them from the crate Cody had loaned me. Both cautiously climbed from the crate and found their way to the food bowls and water. We sat watching them as we ate our Chinese food. They really were banged up, but they seemed really sweet. After we ate, I went into the stall and sat down with them. I sat quietly and let them come up to me. It took less than thirty minutes for them to make their way over to me, where they both curled up against my leg and fell asleep. I carefully extricated myself from the stall and closed the door. We headed for the cabin, knowing they would be good for the night. Jordan finished up some homework while Kasey and I watch another episode of *Game of Thrones*. We already had Arryn, so we decided the new pigs would be Lannister and Baratheon.

Everyone was up early the next morning. We headed out to check on Lanny and Barry and found them still sleeping. We added the antibiotics to the food and placed the bowls down for them. They stirred when we opened the stall door and quickly finished their breakfast. Jordan and Kasey joined me in the stall, and Lanny and Barry welcomed the attention. After morning chores, Kasey left to take Jordan to school, and I put a call in to Ben.

When Ben called back, I explained our three new additions and asked if he had any ideas. He told me he would get back to me later in the day. He wanted to check with his buddy that had provided us with the hut. When he called back later in the evening, he had secured a shell of a small cabin that he could convert into a house for the pigs. He had all kinds of ideas when I told him the pigs' names. He immediately recognized the names as great houses from *Game of Thrones*. He also wanted to know if we were going to get six more pigs so we had all the houses. I assured him we already had more than enough. I told him I trusted him to make something wonderful, and we talked about where we could set it up. There was an acre of land, just east of the small barn, that was relatively level. Ben knew exactly where I was talking about, and he said it would take a few weeks, but he would work it in around his other jobs.

It took almost a month before the pig cabin was ready, but it was well worth the wait. He had converted the shell of the cabin into something straight out of *Game of Thrones*. It was simply amazing; the interior was set up with an area where people could go in and sit with the pigs. Arryn, Lanny, and Barry had become favorites of both volunteers and guests, and the volunteers loved taking them for walks. Arryn continued to be the boss, and Lanny and Barry were perfectly happy letting her. Lisa and the volunteers planned a grand opening for the new *Game of Thrones* pig kingdom. Brad and Carla did an article on the pigs' stories to bring awareness to the problem and created a GoFundMe account to help pay for their medical bills and ongoing care. By the day of the grand opening, we already had over $15,000 in the account.

CHAPTER 35

Driving Lessons

Jordan continued to spend a lot of time with me. He seemed comfortable talking to me about a lot of things. He told me about a girl he liked and was not sure about asking her out. He had met her at Homestead, and they hit it off, but he had no idea what to do.

We had been bowling on several occasions, and I suggested we could all go bowling. We could make it a double date, Kasey and me and him with the girl he liked. When he hesitated, I asked him what was wrong. He told me he was nervous. I told him that was normal, and everyone was nervous on a date. He seemed to relax and eventually asked her. She agreed, and I took him shopping for some new clothes. The evening of the date Jordan emerged from his room, and I realized what a nice-looking young man he had grown into. It was not just his appearance; it was his personality. He was compassionate, funny, creative, and all around a good kid. I felt like a proud parent watching their kid grow up. I knew Jordan felt the same way about me, and it was not unusual for him to tell me he loved me. Of course, I told him I loved him too.

Bowling was a lot of fun, and everyone seemed to have a good time. Kasey had to work nights and had to leave from the bowling alley. After we took his date home, I could tell something was on his mind. I asked him if he had a good time, and he smiled and said he had. He was just thinking about dating and the fact that he would never be able to drive. Several of his friends were getting their driver's permit, and I could tell it was bothering him. I told him about Lyft and Uber and how we would figure things out. I got the feeling it was more about the actual driving than anything else.

It took me a couple of days to come up with a plan. I had talked to Kasey, asking if I was crazy; and with a laugh and a shake of the head, the answer was no, I was not crazy, but I had better be careful. I picked a weekday when I knew it would be slow and Jordan would be out early. As soon as morning chores were finished, I asked Jordan to go for a Jeep ride with me. I drove the wrangler out to the middle of one of the unplanted fields. I put the Jeep in park and then got out. I told Jordan to switch seats with me. He sat there for a minute and asked what was going on. I laughed and told him I was giving him driving lessons.

It took a minute for my comment to sink in, and his response was simply, "Are you kidding me?"

I assured him I was not and told him to get in the driver's seat. When he sat down, I had him adjust the seat so he was comfortable and put on his seatbelt. Out of habit, I told him to adjust the mirrors. When he started laughing, I realized what I said and joined in on the laughter. I had him use his hands as I described each of the knobs and switches. I had him feel the gear shift and went over each position. I made sure he was comfortable with the gas and brake pedals. I got in the passenger seat and put on my seatbelt. I asked if he was ready and had him put his foot on the brake. I then had him move the gear shift to drive and take his foot off the brake.

As the Jeep started to roll forward, I saw Jordan tense up. I reached over and put my hand on his shoulder and told him to relax. I told him to put his foot on the gas and gently press down. As the Jeep picked up a little speed, I had Jordan maintain his hand position. It was a large field. I wanted to let him get the feel of driving forward. Once he seemed comfortable, I had him turn to the left by slowly turning the wheel. When we completed a left turn, I had him straighten out the steering wheel, and we continued forward. A little farther, and I had him do a right-hand turn in the same manner. When we were approaching the edge of the field, I had him do a left-hand turn until we were heading back in the direction we had come. I had him increase his speed, and with the windows down, our hair was blowing in the wind. We were going about twenty-five miles per hour, but I was sure to Jordan it felt faster.

We drove around the field for about an hour, with me telling him left turn, right turn, and then went to telling him 90 degrees or 180 degrees, and he was close every time. We were both laughing, and I could feel the joy pouring off of him. I finally had him take his foot off the gas and gently apply the brake. When we stopped, I had him put it park, and when he completed that, he started to undo his seatbelt. I told him he was not finished yet. He still needed to drive in reverse. I asked if he remembered the position for reverse, and he put his foot on the brake and slid into reverse. I had him start of slowly and then slowly increase his speed. When he had mastered driving in reverse, I had him come to a stop again and put it in park.

When we stopped, I asked how he was feeling. He told me it was one of the best days of his life. I told him as we were swapping seats that he had to promise me that he would never do this on his own, and whenever he felt the "need for speed" that he would come get me, and we would find another field for him. He readily agreed, and as soon as we got back to Homestead, he proceeded to tell everyone we ran into that he had driven the Jeep. Kasey acted surprised when he said he had driven the Jeep, and then we all enjoyed his reenactment of the entire experience. Kasey suggested it was time to celebrate with some ice cream, so we drove into Kalispell to visit Sweet Peaks.

CHAPTER 36

AJ

With school out and warmer temperatures, you could often find Jordan and I out riding the trails. He and Thunder were great riding partners. On many occasions, you would find Kasey alongside us on Storm. Storm was a buckskin quarter-horse mare with black mane and tail. She was a tall girl, easily reaching sixteen and a half hands high. She had been a brood mare for the past several years, but it was time for her to enjoy retirement. We had planned on selling her, but the first time Kasey met her, I knew they were meant to be together. Once Lanny and Barry had moved into the pig kingdom, we brought her over to Homestead. People often did a double take when they glanced into the large pasture. Jolie, Storm, Thunder, and Miracle caught their eye, and then right in the middle of all of them stood Dakotah, weighing over one thousand three hundred pounds.

On one of our early morning rides through the woods, I was lost in thought when I noticed Jordan stopping behind me. I heard him ask if I could hear the animal crying. I listened closely but could not hear anything. I circled back to Jordan and listened again. Still nothing. We dismounted and tied the horses to a nearby tree. I asked Jordan what it sounded like, and he said it was a chattering noise. I asked him to show me the direction the noise. He put his hand on my shoulder and turned me toward the sound.

As we walked a little way into the woods, I began hearing the sound. As we got closer, it sounded like the animal was in distress. When we finally found the source, it was a squirrel that had been caught in a trap. I had Jordan stay with the squirrel while I ran back to Jolie to see what I had in the saddlebags. I found my knife and a bag I used to keep dry goods in when we took longer rides. As I got back, I found Jordan close to the squirrel, talking to it. It seemed to have calmed down, but from what I could see, his leg looked bad. I handed Jordan my riding gloves and had him put them on. I explained I was going to try to get the squirrel in the bag, and I would need him to hold it while I pried the trap open. I told him the squirrel would try to bite and to be careful.

Jordan continued to talk to the squirrel while I placed the bag over its head and body. It became aggressive, but Jordan took his hands and placed them on the bag, still talking to the squirrel, telling it that we were only trying to help. It took a few minutes, but I was finally able to pry the trap open with my knife. When his leg was free, he dropped into the bag. Jordan continued to hold the bag and brought it close to his chest. The squirrel must have felt Jordan's intention as it calmed down and allowed Jordan to carry it back to the horses. I pulled up the trap and put it in my saddlebags. I would call the police when we returned. The woods were private property, and it was clearly marked no hunting was permitted.

Jordan handed me the bag so he could mount Thunder, and the squirrel immediately began chattering. Once I handed the bag back to Jordan, it calmed down again, and we made our way back to Homestead. I called Cody and asked if we could bring the squirrel in to the clinic. He said he was out on a call but would be back within an hour. I went and grabbed a small dog carrier from the barn, along with an old towel. I met Jordan on the porch of the cabin, and we opened the bag, letting the squirrel into the carrier.

Once it was secured in the carrier, I had Jordan get some water, and I cut up an apple with some Cheerios and pecans into a small bowl. I carefully handed the squirrel a piece of apple through the wire door, and he took and ate it. I let Jordan hold another piece for him, and he quickly took it as well. I carefully opened the wire door and placed the water and food inside for him. We still had a few minutes before we needed to leave, so I called the police. I gave them the report over the phone and told them we could drop the trap at the police station while we were in town. I sent Kasey a text, and we loaded up the squirrel in the Jeep. We had to wait a few minutes for Cody to arrive, so Jordan and I sat and talked about trapping. I asked what he thought about it, and he said he honestly had never thought about it before. He told me that it sounded cruel and asked why people would put traps out in "our" woods. I smiled at the term "our" woods and told him I did not know. I explained, in some areas, trapping was a way of life, but that was not the case here.

Cody had to tranquilize the squirrel to get a good look at his injury. As I suspected, his leg was severely damaged. Cody said the only option would be to amputate it. The squirrel would need to be kept in a cage while it healed, but he said it should be able to return to the wild afterward. We still had the large dog crate Cody had loaned us for Lanny and Barry, and that should work until we could set him free. The surgery went well, and the following day we brought squirrel back to Homestead. Jordan asked if we could set up the crate in his room. I told him yes, but he would have to remember to keep the door closed because of Tapa and Rebel. Neither had a propensity to chase squirrels, but we did not know what they would do with one inside the cabin.

On the ride back from picking up the squirrel, I asked Jordan what he was going to call it. He thought for a moment and then smiled. He told me he was going to call it AJ. I immediately knew what he was saying. I shook my head and told him no. He then reminded me he got to name it, and AJ was very appropriate. The squirrel was just like his hero. It was strong, brave, and even with one leg, it was going to be amazing. As a tear fell from my eye, I looked over at Jordan and quietly told him okay.

The following week we checked the surrounding woods where the trap had been set and found eight more. Unfortunately, the area was fairly remote, and we were not able to find anything that would lead to a suspect. I did buy several trail cameras to place in and around the area and a few more to place at the various trailheads on our property.

Meanwhile, it seemed AJ was healing nicely. He had managed to figure out climbing the crate with his three legs, and we found out later Jordan had let him out of the crate on several occasions. When Cody gave us the go-ahead, I asked Jordan if he wanted to go with me to release AJ. Jordan really wanted to keep him, but I explained that AJ was a wild animal and deserved to be free, not kept in a cage. He understood but had grown fond of him. We drove near the area of the trail and opened the crate. AJ scampered out and headed for the nearest tree. We said goodbye and drove back to the cabin.

The next morning, as I opened the door, I was met with a chattering three-legged squirrel who rushed past me into the cabin. AJ bolted toward Jordan's room with two dogs in quick pursuit. Jordan did not spend the night, so the room was empty. I managed to get the dogs out and the door shut before I called Jordan to tell him his little buddy had returned and to tell him I was going to get AJ outside, but I wouldn't be surprised if he hung around. I told him I would be by before dinner to pick him up and bring him out to Homestead. I called Dad to tell him I would be over a little later; I had to get a squirrel outside before I left. I walked into Jordan's room and closed the door. AJ stood on the headboard, chattering away. I walked over to the window and opened it and then tried to get AJ to go out. I felt like we were playing football, with AJ the running back and me the tackle. I would go left; he would go the opposite. I would go right; he would again go the opposite. I tried going high, and he ran between my legs. On my next attempt, I reached low to grab him, and the little shit ran down my back and then out the window. I closed the window and tried not to feel like I had just been beat by a squirrel.

After picking up Jordan, we stopped to grab Italian for dinner and took it to the farmhouse. We often had dinner with Dad and Bill, and everyone laughed as I told them about the AJ adventure. A little later we drove to the cabin. As we pulled up and parked, I heard the familiar chattering. When Jordan got out of the Jeep, he called for AJ, who magically appeared and climbed up onto his shoulder. I explained to Jordan that there was no way I was going to have a squirrel living in the cabin. Jordan argued that we already had a squirrel living there for several weeks, and I explained that was for rehab. He took off for the barn with AJ still on his shoulder. I shook my head and went inside. Jordan came in a bit later and said he had made a spot for AJ in the barn. I was not sure where or what he had used as he did not ask for any help, but I knew I would find out soon when I did the evening feed.

I must admit Jordan did a nice job, especially without being able to see. He had taken two pallets and placed them on end up against one of the walls. He had put straw and blankets in the bottom and then took three poles and put them across the top of the pallets and covered that with a blanket, creating a type of roof over one half of the makeshift hut. He set some treats and water on top for AJ. I did not see AJ at all while I was doing evening feed, and I hoped he had returned to the woods. When I reached the door to the cabin and opened it, once again the little shit darted inside. Jordan was in his room, and of course, he made a beeline for him. At least this time the dogs did not give chase. When I reached Jordan's room, AJ sat perched on Jordan's shoulder, and Jordan was wearing a big smile. I asked Jordan to take him back outside, and he obliged by taking him onto the porch. A little later Jordan returned squirrel free.

The next morning I was ready for the little shit when I opened the door, but to my surprise, I was not rushed by a squirrel. I looked around and then closed the door. I walked over to Jordan's room and peaked in. There was Jordan and AJ curled up on the bed. Jordan's window was open. I knew this was a war I could not win, so I closed the door and started on the morning chores. When Jordan joined me a little later, I told him AJ could stay, but he always had to have the ability to leave. Later that week I took a blueprint of a doggie door and created a squirrel door from the outside right into Jordan's room. Even on nights that Jordan stayed at his grandparents, I looked in and found AJ sleeping on Jordan's bed. Tapa and Rebel seemed to accept AJ as part of the family too and eventually stopped chasing him around the house.

CHAPTER 37

Finding Peace

The crowds over the summer continued to grow. The *Game of Thrones* pig kingdom had become a destination, and we had people coming from out of state and even from overseas to visit. We added several people to our volunteer group, and we planned on building some type of visitor center before next season. The animals continued to thrive, and AJ did his best to aggravate me at every turn.

We were approaching the end of July, and I realized it had been five years since that horrible day that changed my life forever. It was hard to explain. Everything was going so well; yet I could not help but think about what had happened. Kasey had picked up on it right away and asked what was on my mind. I tried to explain it, but I really did not understand it myself. Jolie and I would go for long rides, and I just could not shake the feeling. I knew I was probably one of the luckiest people alive, and I should be grateful. I was surrounded by caring and loving people and some of the most-amazing animals.

I finally decided to reach out to Chris and find out when the next veteran's meeting was scheduled. I had not attended regularly for over a year, but we still hosted meetings at Homestead. He told me there was one scheduled the following Tuesday. When I arrived, it was nice seeing some familiar faces. Chris and Shannon were both there, along with David. I was a little surprised to see Mac. He looked great, and I asked him how Gizmo was doing. He told me she was amazing. He told me he had started a new job six months ago, and his life was better than he ever imagined. Chris called for everyone to sit down, but I told Mac that I would like to catch up afterward. He nodded, and we grabbed a couple of chairs.

After the normal business, Chris opened the floor for questions and comments. It took a little while before I said anything, but eventually, I explained to the group how I had been feeling. I wanted to know if any of them experienced the same thing. There were a lot of head nods and agreement, but no one seemed to have any answers. For the second time that night, Mac surprised us when he started to talk. He began talking about himself and the darkness that nearly overtook him. He talked about his buddy's suicide and how he nearly took his own life. He talked a little about Homestead and then Gizmo. He said without her, he would have never made it; that on the days he had thoughts of suicide, he would think of her and who would care for her. She was always by his side and would curl up in a ball, right in the middle of his lap. As he would pet her, he would feel the darkness lift and knew he could make it another day. After a while, he had mostly good days, but there was always something lurking in the back of his mind.

He had my full attention by now. That was exactly how I had been feeling. He went on to say he had started working with a new therapist, and their approach to things was different from those he had dealt with before. The therapist focused on helping him to find his balance and then to be at peace with the world as it was. He laughed and said, at first, he thought it was a bunch of mumbo jumbo; but after a few weeks, he started noticing a difference. They were going back and talking about things that had happened and exactly what had caused his brain trauma. The therapist encouraged him to take the event apart, piece by piece, and go through all the emotions. He was forced to look at all the what-if scenarios and what might or might not have happened. Through all this, he said he was finally able to let go of the anger and realize sometimes things happen. The key was to keep your perspective and balance. If you can accomplish that, he said you would always be at peace within yourself. He said, "Peace is not something that you acquire because of your external circumstances being to your satisfaction. It is a state of mind that endures regardless of circumstance." For him, he said learning to be at peace when the world threw you curveballs enabled him to feel whole again.

I, along with everyone else in the room, sat there in a state of wonder. I had met Mac at one of his low points, and now I was looking at an entirely different person. As soon as the meeting was over, I sought Mac out and asked him his therapist's name. Apparently, I wasn't the only one. We sat and talked for a while, and he asked when I started having the thoughts and nagging feelings. I told him most recently. It was around the five-year anniversary of losing my leg. We continued to talk about how I had been able to find my balance through Jolie and Tapa and more recently through Kasey. He explained that it was because they already had balance, and I could draw my balance from them. He told me it was time to find my own balance and make peace with what had happened five years ago. I thanked him for everything and told him I was going to try.

On the drive home, I thought a lot about what he had said. I knew I would call the therapist the next day. When I got home, Kasey was waiting. We grabbed a couple of beers, and I shared what Mac had said. I loved the fact that I could talk to Kasey without judgment. I think Mac might have been right. Kasey had found the balance.

Early the next morning, before chores, I took Jolie, and we rode out to the cemetery. I sat there and talked to Mom for over an hour. I told her all about the newest additions to Homestead. I told her about Bill moving in with Dad. I told her about David and Lisa, and even AJ. I spent a lot of time telling her about Jordan and then about Kasey. I promised to bring them both to meet her. I then told her about what Mac had said. As I got ready to leave, a two-tailed swallowtail landed on Mom's headstone.

It was mid-August before I could get into the therapist, and the experience was exactly like Mac had described it. I started off going weekly, and now I go once a month. I found there were many life events that I needed to deal with, going all the way back to being bullied for being part Native American. I never had really dealt with

Mom's death and certainly not losing my leg. After each session, I felt a little lighter, and it was near Christmas when I really understood what it meant to find peace.

For Christmas we were having a large party at Homestead. We had several Christmas trees decorating the drive and all the barns. The community Christmas tree continued to grow, and each night we would make the walk down the end of the drive to read what people had written. The animals were the stars of Homestead, and we even had a live nativity scene, although putting that together was a story in itself. Let's just say AJ playing the role of baby Jesus, surrounded by Cotton, Candy, BJ, Oscar, Pinky, Brain, and Dakotah, with Arryn, Lanny, and Barry dressed as the three wise men not only took a lot of work but the disasters, laughter, and pure joy pulling it off is enough to fill another book.

Kasey had officially moved in just before Thanksgiving. Kasey's parents were going to be coming in for Christmas and staying at the farm of Kasey's grandfather. They had asked if we would start getting the farm ready to sell, and we knew that would be a good winter project. Jordan was still splitting his time between Homestead and his grandparents' house, but he would be spending his Christmas break with us. His grandparents would spend Christmas Day with us at the farmhouse.

Homestead's Christmas party was held on December 21, and I could not come close to estimating how many people attended. Once again, Lisa and the volunteers had outdone themselves, and when they arranged for Christmas carolers to show up, it created a Christmas that would outshine any fairy tale. As everyone left for the night, Kasey, Jordan, and I made our way back to the cabin. We had thanked so many people, many I had never met before. I looked around at what we had created, realizing I was finally at peace, knowing Homestead was indeed my sanctuary.

Christmas dinner at the farmhouse on Christmas Day was perfect. Kasey and I took Kasey's parents out to Homestead first, and then Dad and Bill followed with a tour of the ranch. Jordan's grandparents came over early, and his grandmother had so much fun helping in the kitchen. David and Lisa surprised us by finally picking a date for the wedding and asked if they could have it at Homestead. Of course, the answer was yes, and we could not wait for May 23. The day was filled with good food, lots of laughter, and love that could only be experienced with this ragtag group I called family.

As I laid my head down to sleep that night, I was thankful for everything that had happened to me. From the good to the bad, the happy and the sad, everything that I had experienced and everyone I had met along the way had made me into the person I was today, and I could not have felt more blessed.

The last week of the year brought a beautiful snowfall. We spent a quiet New Year's Day tucked in with a fire raging in the fireplace. On January 2 the weather warmed, and I asked Jordan and Kasey to go for a ride with me; there was someone I wanted them to meet. We bundled up and then saddled up. We rode out to the cemetery, and I told them about Mom. They had both heard bits and pieces, but I told them stories she had shared with me about her childhood and all the wonderful memories she had created for me. Just as we arrived, I told them of the two-tailed swallowtail butterfly and the last time I had been here. As we walked toward Mom's grave, I took both Jordan's and Kasey's hands, and when we arrived, I finally had the opportunity to do a proper introduction. I told Mom it was time she met my family. We did not spend long at the cemetery; it was cold. I knew we would not see any butterflies on this trip, but my heart fluttered as if one had settled in my chest. As we rode away, I knew my life, my home, my sanctuary would always be found here in Montana.

Side Note: When I first thought about writing the story of Homestead, this is where I envisioned the book ending. I had found my happily ever after. But the world was not finished with the story of Homestead Sanctuary quite yet.

CHAPTER 38

Pandemic

The beginning of January the news was filled with the story of a new virus that had begun in China. Entire cities in China were being shut down, and this new virus continued to spread. This virus was deadlier than any encountered in our lifetime. People began talking about it and how horrible it must be to have the government mandate and then enforce orders to stay at home.

By the end of the month, the virus COVID-19, short for coronavirus disease 2019, had spread to several other countries, and the World Health Organization declared a global health emergency. I had been in several parts of the world that were being affected by this virus, and I wondered how the people I had met along the way were doing. I remembered last summer having a large group of Chinese visitors at Homestead on their way to visit Glacier National Park.

The first case of COVID-19 in the United States was reported in late January; a man in Washington State had been diagnosed after traveling to Wuhan, China. Several US international airports began screening for the virus. The volunteers began planning a fundraiser, a winter-type festival, to benefit those affected around the world. We planned on hosting the event on February 15, tying into Valentine's Day. We were hoping everyone would "share the love" and donate. The barns were decorated in red hearts, and we would be offering the opportunity to kiss a pig (Liberty), cuddle a cow (Dakotah), and ride a horse.

By mid-February, more cases of the virus were being reported in the United States, and people were beginning to pay closer attention. The event was fun, but I am not sure if the weather or the threat of the virus kept people away. We still managed to make a few thousand dollars to help, and I was proud of the effort the volunteers had put into the event.

With Kasey being a caregiver in a large assisted-living community, we were hearing more about how the virus was affecting senior citizens. The end of February the United States had its first confirmed death in Washington State, and several other cases were now being reported.

As more people became infected, it was apparent the virus was being spread human to human, like the flu. New York was being hit extremely hard, and everyone was beginning to be on edge. Several of our volunteers had family and friends across the country that were being affected. On March 11 the disease had been declared a pandemic, and on March 12 a state of emergency was declared for Montana. I could tell this was taking a toll on Jordan; he was worried. With the technology available, he knew what was happening and was having difficulty processing all the information. We took a ride in the Jeep and talked for a while. He wanted to know how bad it was going to get and if more people he knew were going to die. I was honest with him and told him I had no idea but that we would get through this together. When we got home, we decided we needed to put a plan together.

After speaking to Jordan's grandparents, we decided Jordan would stay at Homestead with us, and his grandparents would stay home. Kasey and I picked up supplies and food for them and took it over. As we shopped, we noticed how people had switched to a hoarding mentality, and some items were in short supply, like toilet paper. I knew better than to tell Bill and Dad that they had to stay home, but I did convince them to let us do the shopping and stock things up. They agreed, and they took care of ordering supplies for the animals and having them delivered.

On March 16 a stay-at-home order was issued for Montana for all nonessential workers. For Homestead, that meant I needed to ask the volunteers to stay home. I realized how serious this was, and for the safety of everyone, I knew it was best. The animals would miss the people, and I knew the people would miss the animals, but there would be better days ahead. Kasey began working longer hours, and I knew the risks were increasing. Kasey felt me struggling. I knew I was having trouble finding my balance, and that was when Kasey reminded me to stay focused and find my peace. Now is the time I should write the story of Homestead. I decided Kasey was right, and I sat down on March 31 and began writing.

Today is April 28, and I am just finishing the story. By telling the story of Homestead, I have found my balance and peace. Do I worry about what is going to happen next? Of course. I worry about Kasey and all the healthcare workers. Am I concerned for my family? Without a doubt. But the one thing I am sure of is, the story of Homestead is far from over. David and Lisa's wedding is on hold for now. Plans for the new visitor center will have to wait. But when we get through this, and we will get through this, nothing can stop us. Homestead will be here as a place for healing, both animals and people. After all, it is called Homestead Sanctuary for a reason.

CPSIA information can be obtained
at www.ICGtesting.com
Printed in the USA
LVHW040327201020
669246LV00003B/237